CRIMSON JOY

Robert B. Parker

CRIMSON JOY

Delacorte
Press

Published by
Delacorte Press
The Bantam Doubleday Dell Publishing Group, Inc.
1 Dag Hammarskjold Plaza
New York, New York 10017

Delacorte Press is a registered trademark of Dell
Publishing, a division of the Bantam Doubleday Dell
Publishing Group, Inc.

Library of Congress Cataloging in Publication Data
Parker, Robert B., 1932–
Crimson joy.

I. Title.
PS3566.A686C7   1988   813'.54   87-33043
ISBN 0-385-29651-7
Limited edition   ISBN 0-385-29668-1
Large-print edition   ISBN 0-385-29672-X

Manufactured in the United States of America

June 1988

10 9   8   7   6   5   4   3   2   1
BG

For all of us

CRIMSON JOY

Sheridan Street in Jamaica Plain goes uphill from Center Street for about two hundred yards, crests, and heads down toward Chestnut Avenue. It's a narrow street, lined with two- and three-family clapboard houses. Many of the houses had been broken up into apartments and a lot of the apartments were occupied by students and recent graduates. The rest by people who worked without a tie.

On a bright, cold day in early March the last shame of winter lingered in the hard compounded mounds of snow and sand, blackened by exhaust and soot.

Frank Belson jammed his car up onto the ice-cluttered sidewalk and parked, the way cops like to, at an angle, with the rear end of the car sticking halfway out into the street. There were two squad cars already parked the same way.

The house in front of us had a small front porch and two

1

front doors. It had been painted a weak green some time ago. The coroner's wagon was in the narrow driveway and yellow scene-of-the-crime tape was strung across the sidewalk on either side of the house. Some neighbors, mostly women with small children, stood around across the street. It was a neighborhood where men worked and women stayed home.

Belson had his badge clipped to his overcoat lapel. The uniformed cop at the door looked at it and nodded and looked at my lapel.

Belson said, "He's okay."

And the cop said, "Sure, Sarge," and we walked past him into the house. There was a front hall with stairs leading to a second-floor apartment, and a door to the left, open into the living room of the first-floor apartment. Inside there were several city employees taking pictures and looking around the room. In the middle of the room, with his coat still on and his arms folded across his chest, was Martin Quirk. He was staring down at a corpse.

Belson said, "Here's Spenser, Lieutenant."

Quirk nodded without looking at me. He continued to stare down at the corpse. I looked too.

We were staring at a black woman, maybe forty to forty-five. She was naked, her hands and feet had been bound with what looked like clothesline, her mouth had been taped shut, and her opaque brown eyes were blank and still. There was blood between her thighs and the hooked rug beneath her was dark with blood. Between her breasts there was a single red rose.

"Another one," I said.

Quirk nodded, still without speaking, staring down at

2

the dead woman. There was no sign of emotion. Belson went and leaned against the doorjamb and peeled the wrapper from a small cheap cigar and put the wrapper in his pocket. He slid the cigar in and out of his mouth, once to moisten it, and then lit it with a kitchen match that he struck with his thumbnail. When he had the cigar glowing he blew out the match and put that in his pocket too. The rest of the cops did what they'd come there to do. No one asked what I was doing there. No one asked Quirk what he was looking at. The room was thick with silence.

Quirk jerked his head at me, said "Frank," and walked out of the room. I followed, and Belson swung off the doorjamb and in behind me as we went out of the house and down the steps to Belson's car. Quirk and I got in the back seat.

"Go down the Jamaicaway, Frank," Quirk said. "Drive around the pond."

Belson eased down the narrow street, took a couple of lefts, and drove onto the Jamaicaway. Quirk leaned back in the seat beside me, clasped his thick hands behind his head, and looked out the window. He had on a poplin raincoat, unbuttoned, a brown Harris tweed jacket, a blue oxford shirt with a button-down collar, a yellow knit tie. I couldn't see his jacket pocket but I knew that the display handkerchief would match the tie.

"The papers are already calling him the Red Rose killer," Quirk said.

"Or her," I said.

"Him," Quirk said. "There've been semen traces at each murder scene."

"At the scene?" I said.

3

"Yeah. Never in the woman. This time on the rug, once on her thigh, once on a couch."

"He masturbated," I said.

"Probably," Quirk said.

"Before or after?"

"Don't know," Quirk said.

Belson drove inbound on the Jamaicaway, with Jamaica Pond on our left. Opposite the pond, on our right, the big, stately houses were touched by the pale spring sun. The houses were less stately than they used to be, and many of them had been taken over by various institutions: private schools, religious orders, elderly housing; some had been condoed.

"It might be a cop," Quirk said.

"Jesus Christ," I said.

Quirk turned his head from the window and looked at me. And nodded.

"He wrote me a letter," Quirk said. He took an envelope out of his inside coat pocket and held it toward me. It was a plain white envelope, the kind they sell in every drugstore. In typescript, it was addressed to Martin Quirk at Quirk's home. There was no return address. I opened it. The paper inside was as nondescript as the envelope. In the same typescript the letter said:

Quirk,
I killed that hooker and the waitress. You better catch
me. I may do it again and I'm a cop.

I looked at the envelope again. It was postmarked in Boston three days ago.

4

"He knows your home address," I said.

"It's in the book," Quirk said.

"Still, he went to the trouble," I said. "He wants you to know he knows your home address."

"Yeah."

"When did you get the letter?" I said.

"After the second killing."

Belson ran a red light at Brookline Avenue and crossed onto the Riverway.

"Could be any cop," I said.

"That's right."

"Could be one of the forensic guys back there now."

"That's right."

"Could be a civilian that wants to confuse the issue."

"That's right."

"Makes it so you can't trust anyone," I said.

"Hardly anyone," Quirk said.

"Except maybe Belson," I said.

Quirk nodded. I smiled at him. Just a big friendly puppy. Quirk looked at me without saying anything. Belson's cigar smelled like someone was cooking a rat.

I said, "Lieutenant, I owe you some things."

Quirk still looked at me without speaking.

"So I figure I'll help you out on this one."

Quirk nodded. "Yeah," he said. "If you want to."

Belson came to Brookline Avenue again and turned right.

"You get full access," Quirk said. "Anything you find out you tell only me or Belson."

"What do you know so far?" I said.

"Three women, all black, all killed the same way, just

5

like you saw. No evidence of sexual assault. Semen traces in the area each time. Same kind of cord used to tie them, same kind of gray duct tape used to gag them. We don't have the bullet yet on this one, but the first two were both shot with a thirty-eight."

"They have anything in common besides black and female?"

"Maybe," Quirk said. "One was a hooker, one was a cocktail waitress at a joint in the Zone."

"How about this one?"

"Don't know yet. Mailman saw her through the front window and called in. Her name was Dolores Taylor."

"Still is," I said.

"I guess so," Quirk said.

"How official am I?" I said.

"You're doing me a favor," Quirk said. "Anyone doesn't cooperate, let me know."

"How about the press?" I said.

"Can't keep it secret," Quirk said. "They'll spot you. They're on this like a dog at a trash can."

"The slime sheets showed up yet? You're not big time unless you get coverage from the national litterbox."

Quirk smiled with no hint of humor. "They're here. Try to stay upwind of them."

"Anyone on this but you and me and Belson?"

"Official investigation proceeds, maybe we'll break it that way. But I got no way to know if the killer's involved on our side. I want somebody outside the department, that I know didn't do it."

"That's the kindest thing you've ever said to me," I said.

Belson stopped for a light near Children's Hospital. The

light changed, and we went past Children's Hospital and turned onto the Jamaicaway.

Quirk said, "Besides what I've told you we don't have anything. No other physical evidence. We'll have a lab analysis on the semen, but it won't tell us much. You can't work backwards from it. We got no fingerprints on the first two, and we won't have any when they get through with this one either. Each woman was killed in her home. The first one, the hooker, in the Faneuil Projects over in Brighton, the second one on Ruggles Street near the hospitals."

"Picked them up, went home with them, and did it," I said.

"Or followed them home," Quirk said, "and pulled a gun and forced them inside, and did it."

"You figure he didn't break in at random because the odds are too long that he'd randomly get three black women," I said.

"Ruggles Street you expect to, but the odds aren't so good in Brighton, and they're less good here," Quirk said.

"And he's probably white," I said.

Quirk said, "Yeah, we figured that. He wants black women but he doesn't go to black neighborhoods to find them. Even Ruggles Street at that end is on the white/ black fringe. Figure he's either scared to go into the black neighborhoods at night, or that he figures he's too noticeable."

Belson turned onto Perkins Street.

"And the letter," I said.

"The lab got shit from the letter," Quirk said, "unless the lab guy doing the testing is the killer."

"You could run it through twice with different techni-
cians," I said.

"And if one of the lab reports turns out to be wrong,
we've got a suspect," Quirk said. "I tried it. The tests were
the same."

"So the lab knows about the letter," I said.

"Which means the whole department will know in a
while. I know. I told them to keep it quiet. But they won't.
It'll get out."

"So in a while everyone will know it's a cop, or might
be."

"Doesn't do much for morale, but I had to check the
letter," Quirk said.

"Anything only you know?" I said.

Belson parked, as before, in front of the house on Sheridan Street.

"No," Quirk said. "The press doesn't know about the
semen, but the department does, which means the press
will."

"Hard to keep a secret," I said.

"Impossible. Cops go home and tell their wives. They
drink beer after a softball game and tell their buddies.
Hell, I tell my wife. You'll tell Susan."

"But she won't pass it on," I said.

"Course not," Quirk said. "Neither will my wife, or
Belson's or anyone else's. But in a week or so it's in the
Globe, and Channel 5 has a film crew out."

"So young and yet so cynical," I said.

Quirk was still staring out the window. "I'm trying to
keep hold of this thing," he said. "The guy isn't going to
stop and the case will turn into Mardi Gras North. Talk

shows, television, newspapers, *Time* and *Newsweek,* the mayor, the governor, the city council, the feminists, the racists, the blacks, the FBI, every victim's state rep, and every harebrain east of the Mississippi River will be fucking around with this thing and getting in the way and souping this asshole up to do it again."

"The guy wants you to catch him," I said.

"Maybe, and maybe he doesn't and maybe it's both," Quirk said.

Belson turned in the front seat and leaned his arm across the top of the seat. The narrow cigar had burned halfway down and gone out, but Belson kept it clamped in his teeth.

"Either way we gotta have our own posse," he said. His thin face was blue-tinged along the jaw with the shadow of a heavy beard.

I nodded. "I may use Hawk," I said.

Quirk nearly smiled for a moment. "Think he can keep from blabbing to the press?" he said.

"As long as Barbara Walters doesn't show up," I said. "Hawk gets light-headed whenever he sees her."

"I guess we'll have to chance it," Quirk said. He got out of the car and Belson drove me home.

2

Susan was wearing black leather pants and low black cowboy boots with blue patterns worked into the leather. She had on a cobalt blouse and some gold chains and two large gold earrings and was sitting in my living room with her feet up on my coffee table, sipping very slowly at champagne with a splash of Midori liqueur. "And what does Quirk want you to do?" she said. The Midori gave the champagne a delicate tint a little greener than chartreuse. Susan spoke with the under rim of the champagne flute resting on her lower lip. Her big dark eyes looked over the top rim.

"He wants me to be someone he can trust," I said. I came around my counter and put a small silver tray on the coffee table in front of her. There was beluga caviar on the tray and a small spoon and some Bremner wafers and six wedges of lemon.

"Yum yum," Susan said. She moved the champagne glass away from her mouth and tipped her head up at me and I kissed her on the mouth.

"No French-kissing," I said. "It muddles the palate."

Susan sipped another gram of champagne and looked at me without comment. I went back to the kitchen and began to pound a couple of boneless chicken thighs with a heavy knife.

"Takes a tough man to make a tender chicken," I said.

"Is Quirk making up a kind of special squad of his own?" Susan said.

"Belson called it a posse. Quirk's own posse," I said.

"Because the killer may be someone in his department?"

"And because his department is going to get eaten up by the circus," I said. "Quirk wants an alternative. He wants someone not on the payroll. He wants somebody the mayor can't boss, and the city council can't threaten. Somebody who's not bucking for captain. He wants someplace to go where it's quiet and he can think."

"Will it be that bad?" Susan said.

"Yes, very soon," I said.

"Have you been involved in something like this before?"

"I was around the Strangler case," I said. "We had psychics and movie producers and dancing chickens in every corner."

I sprinkled some rosemary on the flattened chicken thighs and put them in olive oil and lemon juice to marinate.

"Everyone uses it," Susan said.

11

"Yes," I said. I poured a little of the champagne into my glass. "To get promoted, to get famous, to get rich, to get excited." I drank my champagne and poured some more, and went around the corner to have some caviar.

"How do you afford caviar?" Susan said.

"Low overhead," I said. "I weave my own blackjacks."

"He seems as if he wants to be caught," Susan said.

"The letter. Yeah, probably. But he didn't write it until after the second killing."

"So if he drops clues it may be very slowly," Susan said.

"And a lot of women may die before he drops enough for us to catch him," I said.

Susan took maybe two sturgeon eggs on the tip of the spoon and ate them slowly.

"While we eat caviar," she said.

"And drink champagne," I said. I poured some for her and added a touch of the Midori.

"Shamelessly," Susan said.

"If we drank Moxie and ate Devil Dogs, they'd still die," I said.

"I know."

We each sipped champagne. The leather pants were smooth over Susan's thighs.

"What we know basically is that it's a white guy killing black women. Certainly sounds like a racial crime," I said.

"And the semen traces?" Susan said.

"Certainly sounds like a sexual crime," I said.

"A dysfunctional one," Susan said.

"Because there's no penetration," I said.

"Except with a gun," Susan said. "Think how frightened of women he must be, to tie them up and gag them and render them helpless, and still he cannot actually connect. He can only find sexual expression the way he does."

"Expression?"

"In the original sense," Susan said.

I nodded. "Why black women?" I said.

Susan shook her head. "No way to know," she said. "Psychopaths, and we must assume that we've got one here, have their own logic, a logic rooted in their own symbolism."

"In other words, just because he's white and they're black is not enough reason to assume he's killing them for racial reasons," I said.

"That's right. What the women represent to him, why he needs to treat them as he does, may be a function of their blackness, or their status on the social scale. Or it may be that there is some idiosyncratic association for him that no one else can imagine."

"Like he was traumatized as a child while reading *Black Beauty*?" I said.

Susan smiled, which was always lovely to see. When she smiled her whole self went into it and the tone of her body changed and her coloration livened. "It's usually not that simple, but you have the idea. Given the fear level that must be operating, it could even be that they are so unlike what they symbolize."

"The guy's killed three women; it's hard to sympathize with his fear," I said.

"Yes," Susan said. "But it's worth understanding. Might be worth looking at the bondage. Is it the same in each case? Might it be ritualistic?"

13

"Is there any way to predict what he'll do next?"

"It's what shrinks do worst," Susan said. "We're pretty good at explaining human behavior but we're an embarrassment at predicting it."

"He'll probably kill another black woman," I said.

"Probably," Susan said. "And he'll probably write more letters and eventually you'll catch him."

"Maybe," I said.

"You will," she said. "You're smart and you're tough and your will is absolutely inexhaustible."

"Well," I said, "that's true."

"And I'm going to help you," Susan said.

The timer rang in my kitchen and I got up and went and took the rice out of the oven. I cracked the cover on the casserole so steam could escape, and shut off the oven and turned toward Susan across the counter.

"We are faced with a decision," I said. "I can have supper on the table in ten minutes and we could eat heartily and then fall into bed. But knowing how, as you age, you are inclined toward torpor after a meal, I was wondering how you wished to deal with the question of me jumping on your bones."

Susan had half a glass of champagne and Midori left. She raised it toward the light and gazed through it for a moment and then she drank half of it and lowered the glass and looked at me thoughtfully. Her eyes were so large and dark that they seemed all pupil, as if the iris had disappeared.

"What's for supper?" she said.

"Grilled lemon and rosemary chicken, brown rice with pignolias, assorted fresh vegetables lightly steamed and dressed with Spenser's famous honey-mustard splash, blue corn bread, and a bottle of Iron Horse Chardonnay."

Susan drank the rest of her champagne and leaned forward and put the glass on the coffee table and stood up. She stepped out of the cowboy boots, and unsnapped the leather pants and wiggled out of them and folded them neatly across the back of the wing chair. Then she turned and looked full at me and smiled with all of her energy and said, "I believe it would be best if you jumped on my bones now."

"I knew you'd say that," I said.

"When did you first suspect?" she said.

"When you took your pants off," I said.

"Yes," Susan murmured, her face against mine, "that would be suggestive."

I put my arms around her. "You know what I miss?" I said. "I miss the old days, before pantyhose, when there were garter belts and the flash of thigh above a stocking top."

"Ah, sweet bird of youth," Susan said with her mouth against mine.

"But I'll manage," I said.

And I did.

Later we ate dinner, Susan in one of my blue oxford shirts and me in a pair of stretch-fabric workout pants, the kind with the drawstring at the top. We looked dashing.

"How about therapy?" I said. "Should I start checking shrinks?"

She shook her head. There was a drop of vegetable dressing on her chin and I leaned over and daubed with my napkin. "He probably wouldn't seek therapy," Susan said. "He wouldn't need to, his needs are being fulfilled by the crime. People seek help when they are frustrated, when the pressure is too great to bear."

"Just like me," I said. "Whenever the pressure of tumescence becomes intolerable, I seek you out."

"How lovely to think of it that way," Susan said.

"Well, I'm also motivated by the fact that I love you more than it is possible to say."

"I know," Susan said. "I feel the same about you."

For a moment we were silent, and the connection between us was shimmering and palpable and more changeless than the universe. I raised my wineglass slightly. "Forever," I said.

Her eyes glistened as she looked at me.

"Probably," she said.

3

Red Rose did it again on a wet April day, with the snow finally gone and the slim gold of nature's first green beginning to edge out on some of the shrubs. Dolores Taylor had been an exotic dancer. This one was a singer. Her name was Chantelle, and she played piano and sang in the cocktail lounge of a hotel out near the airport. She'd been killed in one of the hotel rooms and found in the morning by a maid, who was still incoherent from shock.

When Quirk and I got there, there was press of every species jammed into the corridor outside what I heard one television reporter call "the death room." Television lights glared. A big-bellied, red-nosed, thick-necked cop in uniform was guarding the door as we went through. He nodded at Quirk's badge and we went past him into the death room. Behind us I heard the cop say to someone, "Put the goddamned piece up her snatch and pulled the trigger."

Quirk heard him too. He stopped, turned, stepped to the door, and gestured the red-nosed cop inside.

A reporter yelled at him, "Lieutenant, Lieutenant."

Quirk ignored him and closed the door.

Speaking softly, he said to the red-nosed cop, "The victim was a young woman who died terrified and alone. If I ever hear you talk about her like she was a piece of meat, I will personally take that fucking badge off your fucking chest and make you fucking eat it."

The veins in the cop's thick neck swelled and he opened his mouth. Quirk stared at him steadily, standing very close, his raincoat open, his hands stuck in his back pockets.

The rest of the room went about its business. No one even heard Quirk except me and the red-nosed cop. If you didn't see Quirk's eyes, you'd have thought they were talking about lunch.

The red-nosed cop closed his mouth and straightened slightly. "Yes, sir," he said.

Quirk opened the room door again and nodded toward it. The red-nosed cop stepped back to his post. Smartly. Quirk turned and began to speak with the ME. I went to look at the body. There was no reason to, really. There wouldn't be a clue. But you sort of had to look at the body if you were investigating the murder. It was part of how you did it, part maybe of the way you understood what murder was, and what this one had been. I hated it, and like always, I forced myself not to squint or look obliquely. If she could suffer it, I could look at it. I did.

Belson was there, by the window, looking at the room. I'd seen him work before. It was how he did it. He stood

18

and took in the room and absorbed it, and after a while he could tell you everything in the room and explain why it was as it was. His thin face was placid, almost dreamy. The thin wisp of blue smoke from his cigar drifted up past his eyes and curled toward the window.

I walked over and stood beside him, watching the ID people dusting and measuring and photographing.

"Anything different?" I said.

He shook his head, still looking at the room.

"How about lab reports from the other cases?"

"What do you think?" Belson said.

"I think the semen analysis shows he's blood type A, and secretes PGM I," I said.

"Blood type C," Belson said.

"Which means he could be any one of two million males in greater Boston."

Belson still gazed at the room.

"Forty-five percent of all white males are blood type C. Eighty percent of all males secrete PGM when they ejaculate. Fifty-eight percent of them are white. That shit is good for eliminating suspects, but it's useless when you don't have any. He didn't have a vasectomy either."

"Whose room is it?" I said.

"Hers. No booze. No sign the bed had been slept in. No sign the door had been forced."

"I suppose no one heard the shot," I said.

"He probably muffled it with a pillow," Belson said. He inhaled some cigar smoke and let it out slowly. "Her body would have muffled it some."

I nodded.

"We got people checking all the guests. Figure he might

have stayed here. Figure it's hard to walk around carrying twenty feet of rope, a roll of duct tape, and a gun without being noticed."

"Could wrap the rope around your waist," I said, "under your shirt, put a small roll of duct tape in your pocket."

"Yep," Belson said. "Or carry it in a briefcase. But we're checking anyway. You never know."

"She tied the same way?"

"I haven't compared the photos and the write-ups," Belson said, "but it looks the same."

"We should check that," I said. Belson nodded. Quirk came to stand with us.

"Hotel staff," Quirk said. "Guests, people drinking in the bar?"

"Dino's collecting all the credit card receipts," Belson said. "Richie's got the staff, O'Donnell and Rourke got the guests."

"Parking?" Quirk said.

"Unattended," Belson said. "We got the registration of everything that's in the lot, but we got no way to know who was there and left."

"Okay. I'll talk with the press," Quirk said. "We got someplace set aside?"

"The ballroom, second floor."

Quirk nodded and moved toward the door. I went with him. "They've heard about you," Quirk said as we went down in the elevator. "You may as well be around while they ask me about you."

There were folding chairs in the ballroom and maybe two dozen reporters. Most of those in the hallway upstairs had moved down here. Television lights had been set up and aimed at a speaker's lectern at the front of the room. I leaned against the wall near the door with my arms folded across my chest while Quirk walked to the lectern. He still had his raincoat on. The TV sound men moved closer to the lectern, crouching under camera shot, holding forward long, soft microphones with black foam covering. The press photographers began to snap pictures.

"I'm Lieutenant Martin Quirk and I'm in charge of the investigation," Quirk said. "So far we have no suspects in the killings, which we believe to be related. The commissioner has asked me to assure you that every resource of the department will be placed at my disposal until the killer is apprehended."

Quirk said the stuff about the commissioner the way a child recites the pledge to the flag.

"Any questions?" Quirk said. It was like asking a shark if it was hungry.

"Do you expect the killings to continue, Lieutenant?"

"Probably."

"What steps are you taking to apprehend the killer, Lieutenant?"

"All."

"Lieutenant, is the modus operandi the same for this killing as the others?"

"Yes."

"When do you expect to make an arrest, Lieutenant?"

"As soon as we have a suspect with enough evidence to warrant it."

"Lieutenant, do you have any suspects now?"

"No."

"Is it true, Lieutenant, that the killer may be a policeman?"

"I have an unsigned letter which makes that claim."

"Is it authentic, Lieutenant?"

"I don't know."

"I am told that there was spermatozoa at the scene of each crime, Lieutenant. Is that true? And if so, how did it get there?"

Quirk looked without expression at the questioner for a moment before he answered.

"It is true. We are assuming the killer ejaculated."

"Are you treating this as a racially motivated sequence of crimes, Lieutenant?"

"We don't know the killer. We don't know why he kills. We thought it prudent to hold judgment until we did."

"But, Lieutenant, isn't it odd that all the victims are black?"

"Yes."

"And yet, Lieutenant, you are not prepared to say it's racial?"

"No."

"Isn't that denying the obvious, Lieutenant?"

"No."

"Is it true, Lieutenant, that a Boston private detective is assisting you on this case?"

"Yes."

"Is he being paid with city funds, Lieutenant?"

"No."

"Who is paying him, sir?"

"No one. It's a charitable action on his part."

"Is it because you don't trust your colleagues, Lieutenant?"

"No."

"What is his name, Lieutenant?"

"Spenser. He's back there by the door," Quirk said. "I'm sure he'll enjoy talking with you."

Then Quirk stepped down from the lectern and walked through the reporters and past me, out the door. As he passed me, he said, "Enjoy."

4

On Wednesday morning there was a profile of me in the
Globe. PRIVATE EYE ON RED ROSE CASE, it said. It mentioned that I'd been involved in a number of cases, that I'd
had a longtime relationship with Susan Silverman, a Cambridge psychologist, and that I had once been a boxer. It
neglected to mention that when I smiled, my cheeks dim-
pled sweetly. The press never gets it right.

Wayne Cosgrove called to see if there was anything I
knew that I hadn't told the beat man at the news confer-
ence. I said no. He said would I lie to him. I said yes. And
we hung up. I turned to the sports page and read "Tank
Macnamara," and was checking the "Transactions" listing
when Quirk came in. He was carrying an easel and a
chalkboard, and a large paper bag. I said, "Are you going
to brief me?"

Quirk set up the easel, put the chalkboard on it, and

took a new package of yellow chalk out of his coat pocket and set it on my desk. He took two napkins out of the bag and put them on my desk. Then he got two paper cups of coffee out, and two corn muffins. He put one muffin carefully on each napkin, and sat down in my client chair.

"How's Susan?" he said.

"The usual," I said, "glamorous, smart, hot for me."

Quirk bent the plastic lid of his coffee cup carefully up on one side and twisted out a neat triangle, leaving the rest of the lid in place.

"Hard to understand how someone could be all three," Quirk said.

"You're just sulky because they ran my picture in the *Globe* today and not yours," I said.

Quirk drank a little coffee. "Yeah," he said. "Let's go over this Red Rose thing."

"Sure," I said.

Quirk stood and walked to the chalkboard.

"If you don't mind, I'm going to want to leave this set up here," he said.

"Fine," I said.

Quirk began to write on the board.

Killer

1. Probably white
2. Blood type C
3. No vasectomy
4. Secretes PGM I
5. Ejaculates at scene
6. Victims—black

25

a. Hooker
b. Waitress
c. Exotic dancer
d. Singer

"What else do we know about him?" Quirk said.

"Victims are black," I said. "Scene of crime is white, or mostly white."

"See *1* above," Quirk said.

"What about the victims?" I said. "Pattern?"

"Like from hooker to singer?" Quirk said.

"Might be a kind of progression up the social scale," I said.

"If he thinks like that," Quirk said.

"You got a profile of him from the forensic shrinks yet?" I said.

Quirk shrugged, "Yeah, but what? Rage against women, or rage against blacks, or both. Powerfully repressed sexuality, manifested through the gun; the semen traces may be masturbation, or they may be involuntary ejaculation. Like when he shoots her."

"Jesus Christ," I said.

"Um," Quirk said. "You talk with Susan about this?"

"Yeah."

"What's she got to say?"

"Same sort of stuff. One thing she said is to remember that psychopaths have their own symbolic system and it may not be like other people's."

"So it doesn't necessarily mean that because he kills black women he hates black women," Quirk said.

"Yes, he only hates, or fears, or something, what the black women symbolize."

"She have any thoughts about what it would be?" Quirk said.

"I asked her that," I said. "She gave me the shrink look and said, 'Zee muzzer, vee often look to zee muzzer.'"

"Her too," Quirk said.

"So we should be looking for a cop had trouble with his mom," Quirk said.

"Maybe," I said.

"On a force that's eighty percent Irish," Quirk said.

"Okay," I said, "let's take another approach. Is he really a cop?"

"Why say so if he's not?" Quirk said.

"Why say so if he is?"

Quirk shook his head. "So we're right back to knowing nothing."

"He did know your home address," I said.

"Like I said, it's in the book."

"But not the Boston book," I said. "He had to know to look in the South Suburban listing."

"It's an easy guess," Quirk said. "An Irish name, not living in the city, you look for him on the Irish Riviera."

"Sure, but it means he went to some trouble," I said. "If he wasn't a cop, and didn't know you, it means he had to find out who the officer in charge was, and then track you down through phone books or whatever, all to tell you he's a cop."

"Give him a feeling of power," Quirk said. "Lotta psychos get to feel powerful by learning stuff about the cop that's chasing them."

Quirk stood quietly by the board for a moment. Then he put the chalk down and walked to my desk and sat in my client's chair. My office window was open an inch and the sound of traffic filtered up from Berkeley and Boylston streets. I looked over my shoulder out the window and glanced automatically at the window where Linda Thomas used to be. There was a set of pastel Levolor blinds in there now.

The rain still slid down the window as it had all week. There were flood warnings in western Mass. Clouds hung around the top of the Hancock building, and places where the storm drains had clogged, the water ran over the curbing onto the sidewalk.

I looked back at Quirk. He was staring at his empty coffee cup as he turned it slowly in his thick fingers.

"How about ballistics?" I said.

"Bullets are from the same gun, but we don't know what gun," Quirk said.

"How about taking a sample from every cop?" I said.

"Commissioner says no. Says the union would raise hell. Says it unjustly casts suspicion on every officer, and would impair the function of the department, which is, as you know, to serve and protect our citizens."

Quirk gave the coffee cup a sudden sharp spin with his fingers and scaled it into my wastebasket.

"Probably wouldn't use his own piece anyway," Quirk said.

. . . The tension in his groin was intense.

"She used to compete with me," he said.

"Your mother?" the shrink said.

"Yes. She used to want to shoot baskets with us, stuff like that."

"How old were you?"

"Little kid, 8, 9 maybe."

"And so it was hard to compete with her," *the shrink said.*

"Well, when I was little."

"Difficult for a child to compete with an adult," the shrink said.

"Well, hell, yes, if you're a real little kid it's hard, even if it's a woman."

The tension in his pelvis buzzed along the nerve paths. His breath was shallow.

"But pretty soon, you know, pretty soon I got older and then she couldn't compete with me."

"At least not in basketball," the shrink said.

He'd caught them once, at night, when he went to the bathroom. He heard his mother's voice and stopped and listened. The door wasn't closed entirely.

"For God's sake, George, you're too drunk to even do it."

He heard the bed rustle and the springs jounce.

29

"What am I supposed to do, rub it until you remember what it's for?" she said.

His father's voice was a mumble. There was more movement. He edged closer to the door. And then it was suddenly wide open and his mother was there naked.

"You dirty little pig," she said. He could remember the feeling, the tightness in his stomach, as she dragged him by the hair back to his room and slammed the door. He heard the knob rattle, and when he tried to open it he couldn't. She had tied it shut. He still needed to go to the bathroom and he sat on the floor by the door, needing to go and filled with dread and something else he didn't understand, and cried.

"Momma, momma, momma."

5

I was in my office thinking about whether to go out for a second cup of coffee when Hawk came in without knocking and sat in my client chair and put his Air Jordans on the edge of my desk. He was wearing starched jeans and a double-breasted leather jacket that looked like it had been made from the hide of an Arabian armadillo. He had two coffees in a paper sack. Well, why not. I wouldn't want to offend him.

"Tony Marcus called me today," Hawk said. "Wanted to know if you and me would have lunch with him."

"Lunch?" I said. "With Tony Marcus? What's on for tonight, dinner and dancing with Imelda Marcos?"

"Tony say he can help you with the Red Rose thing."

"Why?"

Hawk shrugged. "Don't like it that some guy's killing black women."

"Tony's become an activist?"

"Tony been making his living from black women all his life," Hawk said. "Maybe he don't like seeing the pool depleted."

"So why send you?"

"Tony think you don't like him. Think maybe he send one of his own, ah, employees, you might whack him."

"Okay, where we eating?" I said.

"Tony likes the Legal Seafood in Park Square."

"Me too," I said. "What time?"

"Noon."

"You think Tony knows something?"

Hawk shook his head. "Think he wants to see if you know something."

"Gonna be a quiet lunch," I said.

Legal served the best seafood in the city and they didn't make you dress up to eat it. Marcus was there when Hawk and I arrived, sitting at a table with a smooth-faced blond woman who wore lavender lipstick and her hair pulled back on one side. Marcus had a fat neck and a big mustache and a short black Afro touched with gray, and he looked sort of soft. The look was deceptive. He had forced himself on the Irish and Italian mob in Boston and taken away the black community. Nothing much happened in Roxbury and along Blue Hill Avenue that Tony didn't get some of. Black Boston was pretty much his and there wasn't anything that the white mobs and the cops and the new Jamaicans had been able to do about it. He nodded at the two empty chairs and Hawk and I sat.

"Bloody Marys are good here," Tony said. He had one in

front of him. The blonde had a glass of white wine. The waitress stood beside us.

"Something from the bar?" she said.

I ordered a Sam Adams beer. Hawk ordered a bottle of Cristal champagne.

"Jesus Christ, Hawk," Marcus said.

Hawk smiled without humor or meaning.

"You working with Quirk on this Red Rose thing?" Marcus said. "What do you know that's not in the papers?"

"Nothing," I said. "How bout yourself?"

Marcus shook his head without speaking. The waitress brought my beer and Hawk's champagne and more drinks for Marcus and the blonde. She opened the champagne, poured some for Hawk, and put the rest in a bucket near him. He smiled at her and seemed flustered.

"Do you need a little time with the menus?" she said.

Hawk nodded and smiled again, and she flushed slightly and hustled away.

"Woman's fallen in love with me," Hawk said.

"Who can blame her," I said. The blonde looked puzzled.

"I don't like it that some honkie fruitcake is going around this city wasting black women," Tony said.

I raised one fist and held it for a moment, above my head. Hawk murmured, "Right on, bro," and drank some champagne.

Marcus shook his head. "I don't expect any understanding from a white guy," he said. "But you, Hawk?"

Hawk put his glass down and leaned slightly forward toward Marcus. "Tony," he said, "I ain't black, he ain't white, and you, probably, ain't human. You want to look

33

good down around Grove Hall, that's your business. But don't waste a lot of time with the black brother bullshit."

The waitress came for our order. I ordered Cajun fried squid. Marcus ordered red snapper for himself and the blonde. Hawk ordered scallops.

When the waitress left, Marcus smiled a little bit. He said, "You never been too sentimental, Hawk."

Hawk poured himself a little more champagne.

"So it doesn't matter none what my reasons are," Marcus said. "All I'm saying is, if I can help on this thing, I will. I got a lotta contacts, a lotta resources."

"What makes you so sure the killer's white?" I said.

"What they said in the papers," Marcus said. He finished his Bloody Mary and gestured toward the waitress for another one and a white wine for the blonde. The waitress looked at me. I shook my head. She departed.

"Tony, I don't like you," I said.

Marcus shrugged. He didn't seem disheartened.

"But I'll take any help I can get. The problem is, I don't even know enough to ask an intelligent question. The best guess is that it's a white guy and he's nuts. The stuff you were reading in the *Globe* is as much as I know either. All I can say is, if you hear anything, let me know. And if you catch the guy . . ." I shrugged.

"We catch the guy, we going to kill him," Marcus said.

"Okay by me," I said. "You clipped people for lots worse reasons."

The food came. As always at Legal, it came as it was prepared, so my squid and Hawk's scallops came before the red snapper.

"Go ahead, eat," Marcus said.

34

"You think he's really a cop?" Marcus said.

"Yes," I said.

"Maybe you should let it be known that Tony Marcus is interested in this case. Might make him think twice."

I looked at Hawk. He smiled happily and ate a scallop.

"The guy who's doing this hasn't thought once," I said. "It's got nothing to do with thinking. He's probably doing it because he needs to. He isn't going to be frightened off."

"Might make the papers, though," Hawk said, almost to himself.

"Black Crime Lord volunteers to help trap Red Rose Killer."

"Good PR," I said. "Federal strike force got a tap on you or something?"

The red snapper arrived. Marcus took a bite; nodded to himself. "Whatever," he said, "just remember Tony Marcus is available with the full resources of the organization."

"Your whores are scared," I said.

Marcus frowned.

"That's what it is. Your whores aren't willing to take a chance with a white hunter anymore because it might be old Red Rose."

Marcus grinned, genuinely, and kept chewing on his redfish.

"It's hurting business," Hawk said.

"Worst thing happen on the street since AIDS," Marcus said.

"Good to find a real reason," I said.

"Maybe there's more than one real reason," Marcus said.

Hawk and I were finished eating. Hawk took the champagne bottle out of the ice bucket. It was still half full. He put it back. Both of us stood up.

"I hear anything, Tony, I'll let you know," I said. "And vice versa."

Marcus nodded and put out his hand. I didn't shake it. Neither did Hawk.

"Finish the champagne, Tony," Hawk said. "Goes good with six Bloody Marys."

We turned and walked away. I heard Marcus mutter to the blonde, "The fucking odd couple."

I looked back. Tony was watching us leave and the blonde was pouring Hawk's champagne into her empty wineglass and smiling automatically.

6

On Wednesday morning I got an audio tape in the mail. There was no return address on the package, and nothing on the label of the tape. I went over to the office stereo and took out my Ben Webster tape and put in the new one. Over the kind of speakers that Ben Webster deserved I heard a man's voice speaking in a harsh whisper.

Spenser, how are you? I'm the guy you're all looking for. I'm the guy doing those colored girls. You think you can find me? I don't think so. I don't think you're good enough. I think if you ever come up against me you're going to be up against something you can't handle. And maybe while you're looking for me, I'll be looking for you. And I know who *you* are.

The whisper was probably to disguise his voice. The phrasing was that of a man reading something he'd written out earlier. There was no background noise, no telltale sounds of a clock chiming on the coast of Bohemia or the whinny of a zebra that lived only in the Tasmanian central plain.

I played the tape again. It sounded just the same. I rewound it and played it again. After the fifth run-through I acceded to the fact that there wasn't anything to hear that I hadn't heard the first time. I called Quirk to tell him what I had, and he said Belson would come by and get it.

Which he did.

When he was gone I added up what I knew about the Red Rose killer. It came out to approximately nothing. Whatever had made him write Quirk had made him send me the tape. Or maybe it had. Or maybe there was an entirely other reason. Or maybe it wasn't really him. Maybe it was a crank. Or maybe Quirk's letter was from a crank. Or maybe both.

I'd learned over the years how to react when I ran into a mystery wrapped in an enigma. I locked the office and went down to the Harbor Health Club.

When I started working out there the Harbor Health Club was a working gym for fighters on the waterfront. The waterfront was run-down and warehousey, and Henry Cimoli, who ran the place, wore sweatshirts and Keds. Now the waterfront glistened with urban renaissance and the Harbor Health Club glistened with shiny leotards and Henry had on white satin sweats and Reeboks. A picture window looked out on the harbor and rows of Nautilus and high-tech Kaiser Cams, sparkling with chrome, lined the wall opposite. The Kaisers used compressed air for resistance and enabled you to do bench presses sitting up. There was probably a clear advantage to doing bench presses sitting up, and I hadn't the smarts to figure out what it was. I mused on this while I did 15 reps at 250. I was trying for more reps and less weight as the sweet bird of youth began to flutter. Across from the weight room, an aerobics class was under way in the exercise room. I mused on this while I rested between sets on the bench press. I mused that I had never seen a woman who looked good in leotards, with the possible exception of Gelsey Kirkland. Susan wore sweats and a T-shirt when she worked out. I mused that most men when they started working with weights tried to lift too much and cheated, and that most women did the exercise exactly as they should but didn't try hard. I mused that the Red Rose killer had threatened me, maybe, and wondered why. He hadn't threatened Quirk. He'd asked Quirk, in effect, for help. But me he'd challenged. Me he'd threatened. I mused that this was an interesting insight into Red Rose, but I also mused that I had no idea what it meant. Henry came into the weight room with a woman in full uniform. She wore a lavender leotard, with matching Nikes, and sloppy socks in a darker lavender. Over the leotard she wore a white sort of G-string that looked rather like a diaper. She had on white wristbands and a white headband, and a lavender ribbon tied in her hair. She had managed, somehow, to achieve a condition simultaneously thin and flabby. I was fascinated, and while I did my second set of bench presses sitting up I speculated on how you could be thin and flabby at the same time, and decided that as your body mustered up the energy to add an ounce of weight it was so spent

39

having done so that the ounce turned instantly to flab. Henry smiled kindly and nodded at the machine for hamstrings. The woman got on backwards. Henry smiled even more kindly and got her turned around.

"Heels under here," Henry said. "Now curl the legs up slowly."

"What do you mean curl?" the woman said.

"Try to touch your, ah, backside with your heel," Henry said.

Henry had removed his glistening white warm-up jacket and his little upper body in its tight T-shirt looked like a clenched fist.

"I can't," the woman said. "It's too heavy."

"It's as light as it goes, ma'am," Henry said, and smiled kindly some more. "Maybe you could try a little harder."

"It hurts," she said.

"Well"—Henry laughed kindly— "like they say, ma'am, no pain, no gain."

"I don't understand what that means," she said.

I knew Henry knew I was there. But he wouldn't look at me.

"Here," Henry said, "I'll help you. Now, curl your legs up, I'll give a push. There."

"Is that enough?" she said.

"No," Henry said. "Usually we like people to start with eight repetitions and work up to twelve and then add some resistance."

"Eight what?"

"Do it eight times."

"I've already done it once."

"Right, only seven more."

"I can't do seven more."

"I'll give you a start," Henry said.

Henry curled the machine up, bringing the woman's legs up to within maybe a foot of her thin, flaccid butt.

"Ow," she said.

Henry looked at the front desk. There was a trim young woman in white sweats there. Henry jabbed his finger at her and thumbed toward himself. She came over.

"There," Henry said to the woman. "I've got you started; Janie will take you through the rest of the machines."

The woman said, "I don't want to do all those machines today."

Janie said, "It'll be fun once you get started, you'll see." She glanced at Henry. There was no kindness in her glance. I was on the lat machine, and as Henry and Janie exchanged their glances I turned around and did a handstand on the seat of the lat pull down machine, so that I was effectively on it upside down.

"Excuse me, Mr. Cimoli," I said. "Am I doing this right?"

Henry turned and stared at me for a moment with no change of expression.

"Why, yes, sir," Henry said, and smiled kindly. "You're doing just fine." He stepped nearer to me and said more softly, but just as kindly, "Now, why don't you pull the weight down with your dick," and moved off toward the front desk.

I finished up on the weights and put in an hour in the boxing room. It was Henry's last gesture to his roots. He kept a speed bag and heavy bag and a couple of jump ropes in a small room that could have been used for Jacuzzi space. I did ten 3-minute rounds, alternating on the heavy bag and, every third round, the speed bag, and then skipped rope for fifteen minutes. I tried to time the speed bag stuff for when a young woman walked by on her way from aerobics. I could still make the speed bag dance.

When I got through with the jump rope I was blowing my breath and soaked with sweat. I felt like a squeezed-out sponge. When I was fighting I used to be good in the late rounds. The other guy was getting arm-weary and I was still full of starch.

I was out of the shower and getting dressed when Henry came in.

"Used to be simple," Henry said. "I'd train hard and then when I was ready, I'd go in the ring and Willie Pep or Sandy Saddler would ring my chimes for me, and I'd go home and in a few days I'd start training again."

"That woman didn't seem to have the killer instinct about training," I said.

"Half the people who come in here are like that. They want to feel great and look great and not pop a sweat. That woman was bad. But the worst are the guys who always thought jocks were vulgar, you know? And then they get a physical and the doctor says they need exercise. So they come down here wearing black socks and white tennis shoes and say things like 'this machine is rather intimidating,' and you got to practically put their fucking hands on the handles for them. They don't come down and scope things out a little. They don't look at the machine and notice there's probably only one way it can work. They don't watch other people work out for a few minutes and see how they do it. They come in and get on the fucking equipment upside down and flap their fucking arms like a fucking cocka doodle fucking do until you go over and say, 'Perhaps it would work better if you did it this way.' "

I was dressed by the time Henry got through and was buttoning up my shirt.

"Feel better?" I said.

Henry grinned. "On the other hand, I haven't had any stitches in my lip lately."

"Good point," I said.

It was a very fine spring day as I walked back to my office, across the Common. I was wearing chinos and white Reeboks and my leather jacket and a white shirt with a wide lavender stripe, which was as daring as I got. I felt strong and clean, like I always did after I worked out; and this evening, before dinner, two beers would taste exactly the way they should.

Be nice to know why the Red Rose killer had threatened me.

7

I was in Quirk's office at 9:40 on a Thursday morning, trying to figure out why Red Rose had threatened me.

"Maybe it's a variation on 'Catch me before I do it again,' " Quirk said. "Maybe sort of a challenge to get us working harder."

"You heard the tape," I said. "Is that what it sounds like to you?"

"No," Quirk said. "It sounds like he feels hostile toward you."

Quirk had his coat off and hanging neatly on a hanger from his coat rack. His cuffs were turned back on his white shirt. He was wearing a pink silk tie at half-mast and his starched collar was open. As he talked he leaned back in his swivel chair and locked his hands behind his head. His biceps swelled against the sleeves of his shirt.

"Why would he be hostile toward you?" Quirk said.

"Why would anyone?" I said.

Quirk grunted.

"Maybe he knows you," he said.

"And doesn't like me," I said.

"Hard as it is to believe," Quirk said.

"Well," I said, "the man is a psychopath."

"Cops who know and dislike you are not as scarce as hen's teeth," Quirk said.

" 'Course maybe he's not a cop and maybe he doesn't know me and maybe something else is going on," I said. "Susan keeps reminding me that we're not dealing with two plus two here."

A uniformed desk cop came and knocked on Quirk's glass door. Quirk nodded and the cop opened it and said, "Superintendent Clancy, Lieutenant, with some people." Quirk nodded again and the cop went away, leaving the door ajar.

"Deputy Superintendent," Quirk said. "Community Relations. It'll be a group of citizens urging me to catch Red Rose."

I started to get up. Quirk shook his head. "Stick around," he said. "Remind you of why you quit the cops."

I sat back down.

Clancy came in with four people, two blacks, two whites. One of the whites was a woman. Clancy was a small, neat man with a face like a mole. He wore a white shirt with epaulets and a blue cap with gold braid. His shield was polished and shiny on his shirt, and he wore the short handgun high on his belt that headquarters types considered status. His trousers were creased, and his shoes gleamed with a spray-can shine. "Reverend Trenton,"

Clancy said, introducing one of the black men. "Representative Rashad," he said, "and Mr. Tuttle from the Christian United Action Committee, and Ms. Quince from the Friends of Liberty."

Quirk said, "How do you do," and all of them except Quirk looked at me. Quirk ignored it.

"What can I do for you?" Quirk said.

Rashad, the state representative, said, "Commissioner Wilson said you were the one to brief us on this series of racial murders plaguing the community."

"Last year," Quirk said, "thirty-six black people were killed in this city. Nobody came around for a briefing. Nobody called them racial murders."

"Don't be evasive, Lieutenant," Rashad said. "We wish to know the progress you're making on this grisly matter." A man of substance, old Rashad, a man used to being a public presence, prepared to take no guff from a mid-level functionary on the police force. It gave me goose pimples just to watch him.

"You read the papers?" Quirk said.

"Of course," Rashad said. His hair was a close-cropped Afro. His mustache was carefully trimmed. He wore a dark blue suit and a white shirt with long collar points, and a blue-and-red-striped tie. Around his neck was a gold chain and from it a gold medallion hung on his chest, on top of the tie. On the medallion was the raised profile of an African.

"That's the progress we're making," Quirk said.

The white woman, Ms. Quince, leaned slightly forward. She was scowling with concentration.

46

"You know nothing that hasn't been reported in the papers?" she said.

"Just about," Quirk said.

"Not good enough, Lieutenant," Rashad said.

"No," Ms. Quince said. "We wish to know everything."

"Why?" Quirk said.

Ms. Quince opened her mouth and closed it and looked at Rashad.

Clancy said, "Lieutenant Quirk."

Rashad said, "That's all right, Jerry, I can handle the Lieutenant."

Tuttle spoke for the first time. "Lieutenant, I would hate to have to report to Pat Wilson that you were uncooperative."

Quirk was quiet.

It was Reverend Trenton's turn. He spoke very softly. "We are here, Lieutenant Quirk, to ascertain if the police are doing everything possible on this matter. It is a matter of great concern to the black community, to women, to every one of us who opposes racism in this city."

"And sexism," Ms. Quince said.

"And murder," Quirk said. "And the misuse of clothesline."

"Lieutenant," Ms. Quince said. "That is uncalled for."

Quirk nodded. "Sure it is, Ms. Quince. I apologize. But the thing is, your visit is uncalled for too."

Rashad said, "Every citizen of this community has the right to hold you accountable."

"Sure," Quirk said.

"And there is a vicious racist, sexist killer out there, a

47

self-admitted member of your department. We want answers, not smart remarks, and we want them now."

"You may have to settle for smart remarks," Quirk said. "Because I don't have any answers."

Clancy said, "Martin, there's no need to be angry."

"The hell there isn't," Quirk said. "They come in here to be sure I'm doing my job, like I'd forget about it if they didn't."

"Lieutenant," Trenton said, "the black community cannot be blamed for viewing the police with suspicion. How assiduous have you been in the past in solving what I've heard some of you call a 'shine' killing?"

I saw Quirk take a long breath. He let his chair tilt forward and put his hand flat on his desktop.

"Reverend," he said, "I am a professional homicide investigator. I've been one for twenty-seven years. I try to solve every murder, and catch every murderer, because I am employed to do that, and because I want to do that. I do that whether anyone is watching me or not, whether the victim is black or white, male or female; whether the commissioner wants me to or you want me to or God wants me to."

Quirk paused. No one spoke.

"Now, you people," Quirk said, "you people are not employed to catch murderers, and if you were employed to do it, you wouldn't know how. But here you are. If you can be honest with yourselves, you know that coming here won't catch the murderer. You're here so that you can tell your voters or your parishioners or your members that you're on top of things and that you are, therefore, the cat's ass."

When Quirk stopped speaking there was enough silence in the room to walk on.

Finally Rashad said, "Well, clearly, with that attitude there is little point in continuing."

Quirk smiled pleasantly.

Tuttle looked at me. "I will be reporting this meeting to Commissioner Pat Wilson," he said. "Might I know who you are?"

"Orotund Vowel," I said. "I'm the lieutenant's elocution teacher."

Tuttle stared at me. He knew he was being kidded but he didn't know what to say. Finally he turned and led them out.

"Orotund Vowel?" Quirk said.

I shrugged.

"You're a strange bastard," he said.

". . . I was hers all the time I was a kid," he was saying.

"Her what?" the therapist said.

"What do you mean, 'her what'? I was her son."

The therapist nodded.

He wanted to say more about what he was. "I was her only child, you know, she worried about me all the time."

"How do you know she worried?" the shrink said.

Christ, couldn't she figure anything out? "She said so," he said, "and when I did stuff that worried her she'd get, like, sick."

"Sick?" the shrink said.

"Yeah, she'd lie on the couch and not talk all day and her face would have this look, like she was having cramps or something. You know, like broads get when they're having their period." He felt the tingle of daring and guilt when he said it.

"Like mean, you know. Bitchy."

"What does bitchy mean to you?" the shrink said.

"It means crabby, it means, you know, not talking to you, being mad at you, not . . . not loving you. Not being nice to you."

The shrink nodded.

"If I'd come home late for supper or hang around with the guys or go out." He could feel the tightening in his throat and the way his nose began to tingle.

50

"Go out?" the shrink said.

"With girls," he said. *His eyes were filling. He felt himself burning with frustration and shame. "She told me that every girl was going to take me for all they could get." He fought the hot crying. He turned his head.*

The shrink said, "Let it come. Let's see what comes with it."

Like hell. He wasn't going to cry here. His mother had never caught him crying. He held his head down and forced his breath in and out. In his groin he could feel the pressure.

"I can control myself," he said.

"Always?" the shrink said.

He felt a trill of fear.

"Absolutely," he said.

"Control is important," the shrink said.

"You lose control," he said, *"you lose yourself."*

The shrink waited.

"You get controlled," he said. *"You don't control yourself, people control you."*

"Then they could take you," the shrink said, *"for all they could get."*

He wanted to speak and couldn't. He felt as if he'd pushed something aside. He felt shaky now. Deep breath. Let it out. His arm muscles were bunched, and he pressed with his elbows against the arms of the chair.

"My mother always used to say that," he said.

The shrink nodded.

8

The next woman was a schoolteacher, killed in her own apartment on Park Drive overlooking The Fenway. It was Saturday, lunchtime. Quirk and Belson and I looked at the murder scene again. It was as before. The rope. The tape. The blood. One of the precinct detectives was reading aloud from a notebook to Belson.

"Name's Emmeline Washburn," he said. "Teaches at the Luther Burbank Middle School. Seventh grade. Forty-three years old, separated from her husband, lives alone. Husband's over there." He nodded to a black man sitting motionless on an uncomfortable red couch, staring at nothing. "Emmeline went to the movies with a friend, lives on Gainsborough Street, Deirdre Simmons. She left Deirdre at about ten-fifteen at her place, and intended to walk home. Husband came by this morning to have lunch with her and found her. He hasn't been able to say much.

ME hasn't established time of death yet. But she's in rigor. MO seems just like the other four.

Quirk said, "You establish an alibi on the husband yet?"

The detective shook his head. "He's in bad shape, Lieutenant. All I got so far is, he found her."

Quirk said, "I'll talk to him," and walked over to where the man was sitting. "I'm Martin Quirk," he said. "I'm in charge of homicide."

"Washburn," the husband said, "Raymond Washburn."

He didn't look up at Quirk. He didn't look down at the dead woman. He simply fixed on the middle distance.

"I'm sorry," Quirk said.

Washburn nodded. "We were going to put it back together," he said. "We'd been separated a year and we'd been seeing a counselor and it was working and we were going to put it back together."

As he spoke, his body suddenly went limp and he began slowly to lean forward on the couch. Quirk dropped to one knee and caught him as Washburn pitched off the couch. Washburn looked to weigh maybe 190 pounds, and Quirk had to steady himself a moment as he caught the dead weight. Then without apparent effort he stood, his arms around Washburn. Washburn wasn't out. As Quirk straightened I could see him staring blankly over Quirk's shoulder. Then he began to cry. It sounded like the sobs were being twisted out of him. Quirk held Washburn and let him cry until he stopped. Then Quirk eased him back on the couch. Washburn slumped when Quirk let go of him, as if there were no strength in him. His eyes were swollen and his face was wet.

Quirk looked at one of the EMTs that had come with the ambulance. "He'll need help," Quirk said.

"We'll take him down to City," the EMT said, "let one of the doctors talk with him."

Quirk nodded. He looked at me.

"You got any thoughts?" he said.

"No."

"Belson?"

"No."

"Me either," Quirk said. "Let's get the fuck out of here."

We went to my office. I sat at my desk. Quirk sat across, and Belson stood, as he almost always did, leaning against the wall. The office had a closed-up smell. I opened the window and the sparse weekend traffic noise drifted up.

"Could be a copycat," Belson said. "Guy wants to do his wife in, covers it up by making it look like Red Rose, except there's no semen."

"Scene looked authentic," Quirk said, "otherwise."

"It's all been in the papers," Belson said.

"Takes a special guy," I said. "To murder his wife and then deposit semen stains on the rug."

Belson shrugged.

"He was grief-stricken," Quirk said, "but that doesn't mean he didn't do it."

"Got the name of the counselor?" I said.

"Yeah, woman in the South End," Belson said, "Rebecca Stimpson, MSW."

"I'll ask Susan to call her," I said.

"Frank," Quirk said, "go over the crime scene, everything, compare it with the other killings."

Belson nodded.

"And we should get a report on the media coverage. See exactly what it's possible to know about Red Rose from the papers. If this isn't a copycat, there will be one later."

Belson nodded.

"Newspapers, TV, radio, everything."

"Take some time, Lieutenant," Belson said.

"We got nothing else to do," Quirk said.

"Other people get killed in this city," Belson said.

"They wait their turn," Quirk said. "I am going to catch this motherfucker."

From the intersection below my office window a horn brayed.

"Spenser," Quirk said, "I want you to backtrack each case. Start with the first murder. Go through it just like it was brand-new. Talk to everyone involved, read the evidence file and the forensic stuff, treat it like no one ever looked at it before."

"We need a pattern," I said.

"Black women, over forty, living in racially mixed or fringe neighborhoods. One hooker, one cocktail waitress, one dancer, one singer, one teacher," Belson said.

"Up the social scale?" Quirk said.

"If you think singers rank higher than dancers," I said.

"Or he thinks so."

"Over forty," I said.

"Yes," Belson said. "Royette Chambers, the hooker, was forty-one. Chantelle was forty-six. The other three were in between."

"That's a fairly tight age-cluster," I said.

"Especially the hooker," Quirk said. "Forty-one's old for a hooker."

"So why does he only kill women in their forties?" I said. "Five times, it can't be an accident."

"Zee muzzer," Quirk said. "We usually look to zee muzzer."

9

Routine is routine, repetitious details endlessly pursued. I talked with the relatives of the victims, all of whom were bitter and saddened and outraged. All of whom felt that racism had caused their daughter, sister, mother, wife, to die; all of whom had talked before with policemen; and all of whom resented talking with another honkie who was pretending to care while he covered up for the white establishment, which harbored the killer. The bereaved are not necessarily smarter than anyone else.

In three days of this I learned absolutely nothing that the cops didn't already know.

"My daughter was a good girl, mister. She didn't do nothin so someone should kill her."

"Nobody wanted to kill my sister, man. She was a nice lady. She was working regular. She was helping out at home. You got no business trying to say it's her fault."

The hooker had no bereaved kin that we could find. I talked with her pimp. He was taller than I was and twenty pounds slimmer, with close-cropped hair and a one-inch part scribed in the middle. He had on a white tank top and maroon sweats and black high-top Reeboks. There were five or six small gold earrings in the lobe and up the outer curve of his left ear.

"I catch the motherfucker, I'll cut his ass in two," the pimp said.

"You'll have to take a number," I said. "Any thoughts who it might be?"

"Some kinky white john," the pimp said, staring at me.

"We were sort of guessing that too," I said. "You have any special kinky white john in mind?"

The pimp shrugged. "Most of them kinky, man, they down here cruising for hookers."

"Any that complained about bondage, stuff like that?"

"Complain, man? Shit. Hookers don't complain, get slapped upside the fucking head they start complaining. They do what the john wants and afterwards they gimme the money."

"Works out swell for them, doesn't it."

"Whores is whores, man. Ain't my doing."

"You hear any talk," I said, "any stories about guys into bondage, s and m, whatever?"

"Shit, man, I said all this already. Sure there's johns everybody knows about. Like handcuffs, gags."

"Ropes?" I said.

"Ropes, man, inner tubes, fucking anchor chains. Guys that like being spanked. Guys that like spanking. Guys that like rubber underwear. What you want, I know johns do all that shit."

"And you told the cops about them?"

"I give them every name I know, man. I don't like my whores getting clipped, you know. Makes me look bad. Costs me money. I want the motherfucker caught."

"Everybody wants the motherfucker caught," I said.

"Yeah, sure. Everybody killing themselves to catch some guy shot a black hooker."

"And four others."

"I hoping he does some white broad in shopping from Wellesley Hills, man," the pimp said. "Then we see some action."

"What do you call this?" I said.

"This? You here talking with me? Asking me about kinky johns? That ain't action, man, that's blowing fucking smoke, man. That say, 'Hey, we down here looking for who killing you jigaboos, boy. We trying.' Shit."

"You got any suggestions for action?"

"Not to you, man. We gonna catch the motherfucker one day and we gonna kill the motherfucker."

"We?"

"That's right, man, motherfucking we. People of fucking color, man, all right? That's who's gonna give you some action."

"I hope so." I handed him my card. "If it starts," I said, "I'd like to come watch."

He watched me get back in my car and pull away. In the rearview mirror I saw him put the card in his pocket.

10

Susan had her home and office in a big old house on Linnaean Street with a slate mansard roof and a wide front porch. She lived on the second floor, her office and waiting room occupying the half of the first floor to the left of the center entrance hall. I was drinking a bottle of Sam Adams in her living room while she got supper ready.

Getting supper ready in Susan's case meant getting gourmet take-out from Rudi's in Charles Square and reheating as required. She sipped a Diet Coke while she put two chicken breasts with apricot and pistachio stuffing into a red casserole dish to heat in the oven.

She had just finished running two seven-minute miles on the treadmill at her health club and she still wore her black sweat pants and pale blue sweatshirt with the sleeves cut off and the neckline lowered. Her running shoes were Nikes with a purple swoosh.

"I talked with that family counselor today," Susan said.

"Rebecca Stimpson, MSW?"

"Yes. She had been doing some marriage counseling with the Washburns and it was sort of delicate because of confidentiality. But, phrased just right, it's pretty clear that Ms. Stimpson, MSW, did not feel that the Washburns were on the road to reconciliation."

"She have any views on Ray's potential for violence?"

"Not really. She couldn't rule it out, but, as you know, predicting behavior is nearly impossible. Also, in truth Ms. Stimpson doesn't seem like a therapeutic heavyweight."

"She has a master's in social work," I said.

"Yes, and I believe in the value of fuller and more specialized training; but it's not her academic credentials; there are people with Ph.D.'s in psychology and M.D. psychiatrists who aren't therapeutic heavyweights either. It's temperament and, for lack of a better word, simple intelligence. Ms. Stimpson isn't very smart."

"You trust her opinion on Washburn?"

Susan sipped some more Diet Coke. She was tossing a salad composed of endive, julienne of red and yellow peppers, and arugula.

"It's hard to see how she could have been totally misled. She saw them together once a week for several months."

"So if she's not misled, then Ray was lying," I said.

"Not necessarily," Susan said. "Some clients simply want something so badly, they believe it despite everything."

"And if they are forced to see the truth?" I said.

Susan shook her head. "Need is a powerhouse," she said.

"So if the therapist is right . . ." I said.

"Counselor," Susan said. "Not therapist. She wasn't doing therapy."

I grinned. "Correct, just a test to see if you were listening. So if the counselor is right, Raymond is somewhat obsessed, or he is lying. Or the counselor is wrong and it's another Red Rose killing, or both. Or neither, and something we haven't any idea about is going on."

"Fascinating work," Susan said.

"Not unlike your own," I said.

Susan put a loaf of fresh French bread on the table and the salad, served on two glass salad plates.

"Metaphors for life," she said. "Your profession and mine."

I sat at the table beside her.

"You be Simone de Beauvoir," I said, "and I'll be Sartre and we'll consider defining life by living."

Susan smiled and patted my hand with hers. She was still wearing the twisted bandana that she used to hold her hair back when she worked out. On most people I thought it hokey. It looked exactly right on her.

"Eat your fucking salad," she said.

We ate dinner and cleaned up and Susan settled in on the couch beside me to read the *American Journal of Therapeutics*. I watched the Braves and the Reds on cable.

"It's Skip Carey and John Sterling," I said to Susan.

"So?"

"They have a four-man broadcast crew and they do radio and television and they rotate the crew so that the same two guys are never together, and I'm trying to figure out the pattern."

Susan put her magazine down and looked at me silently.

"Really?" she said.

"And," I said, "there's a pattern within the patter in
that each guy does some play-by-play and some color on
both radio and television."

Susan looked at me some more and breathed deeply
and exhaled slowly and went back to her magazine.

By the time the ball game ended Susan had fallen
asleep with her magazine still open before her. I bent
over and picked her up and carried her to bed and put her
down on it. It woke her up and she gazed up at me with
her big eyes.

"What made you think I was sleepy?" she said.

"I'm a trained investigator," I said.

She smiled and made a kissing motion with her mouth. I
bent over and kissed her goodnight and headed home. As
I started down the stairs I heard the front door shut softly.
I froze, listening. The front door should have been locked.
I felt the adrenaline surge and I went down the stairs in a
rush. The front door had been jimmied. I pulled it open.
There was the hint of movement past one of the big
shrubs in Susan's yard. I went over the porch railing and
landed five feet below, next to the shrub. Something,
probably a fist, hit me in the forehead. It wasn't a major
league punch but it jarred me, and a figure burst from
behind the bush and headed up Linnaean Street, toward
Mass. Ave. I went after him with my chimes still ringing. I
had run five miles a day for the last twenty years and
planned to run him down. In a block, I hadn't closed the
gap. He hurdled a waist-high fence on the corner of Ag-

gassiz Street and cut across the lawn and turned up Aggas-
siz. I went over the fence after him and trailed my left leg
and the fence caught it and I sprawled onto the lawn. He
was up the little hill and rounding the corner on Lancaster by the time I got running again, and by the time I got
to Lancaster, he was out of sight. I ran down to Mass. Ave.,
but I ran without enthusiasm because I knew he was gone.
Mass. Ave. leading into Porter Square in Cambridge is
busy in the evening, full of street life and traffic. The
sprinter had disappeared into the crowd. He'd been
dressed in dark clothing and had looked to be a little
shorter than I. He was probably white. He was male. And
he could jump a higher fence than I could. I walked back
to Susan's place with the sweat trickling down my back-
bone and my pulse slowing. Probably the gun had slowed
me down. It was a Colt Python and it probably weighed
two or three pounds with a full load. Otherwise I'd have
soared over the fence.

Susan's front door was still ajar when I got there. I
stepped into the front hall and closed it behind me. The
house was silent. I turned on the hall light. On the hall
table was a long, narrow white box. I opened it. Inside,
cradled in green tissue paper, was a single long-stemmed
red rose.

"Jesus Christ," I said aloud in the empty hallway.

11

When Susan woke up in the morning I was lying in bed beside her with my gun unholstered on the night table. She rolled over and looked at me silently.

"I thought I heard you in the night," she said. Her eyes rested for a moment on the gun.

"On my way out last night I almost caught someone who had broken into your front hallway and left a single red rose for you. I chased him but he got away." I saw no reason to discuss how I fell on my kisser trying to jump the fence. We were lying face-to-face on the bed, Susan's eyes wide and still a little unfocused from sleep.

"You have a bruise on your forehead," she said.

"He hit me from behind a bush," I said.

"Could you identify him?"

"No. It was dark, I only saw him from behind, and he was receding fast."

"You know it was a man."

"Yes. Pretty sure he was white, almost my height. Medium build, tending toward slender, I think."

Susan stared at me some more without moving. Her eyes were focused now, the pupils shrinking as they adjusted to the morning.

"So you came back and spent the night," she said.

"Yes."

"There are several explanations," Susan said.

"True," I said. "It could be someone of your patients, for whatever his reasons."

"It could be someone with a grudge against me," Susan said.

"It could be the Red Rose killer, which could be a variation on number one, above," I said.

"The Red Rose killer could be a patient of mine?"

"Sure. He claims to be a cop. Cops are sort of your specialty."

"Or," Susan said, "it could be directed at you. He knows you're working on this. He must therefore know that you and I are an item."

"Or it could be someone with a grudge against me," I said.

"Or it could be a copycat acting at random," Susan said.

"Long shot," I said. "To hit you at random on a case I'm involved in."

Susan nodded, and looked past me at the alarm clock.

"My God," she said. "I've got my first appointment in an hour and a half."

"That's too soon?" I said.

She was up out of bed and heading for the bathroom.

"Much," she said. And was into the bathroom. The door closed. I heard the shower go on. I got up, put my pants on, buckled my belt, put my gun in its holster, and went to the kitchen. I washed my face and hands and torso at the kitchen sink. Then I started water for coffee.

I was drinking my second cup when Susan appeared in the kitchen, her hair in curlers and some makeup on. She poured hot water over a bag of herbal tea in her cup and let it sit for a minute, looking impatiently at it while it steeped.

I said, "I know that it is nearly impossible to talk while you are performing the morning ablutions, but we have to think about your safety."

Susan snatched the tea bag from the partially steeped tea. "I can't think about that now. I'm in my speeded-up movie mode, and you know what I'm like in that mode."

"Yes," I said.

She took her tea and went back to the bathroom. I sat at the glass brick counter in her kitchen and made two phone calls. One was to Henry Cimoli with a message for Hawk. The second one was to Martin Quirk.

"Someone broke into Susan's front hall and left a single rose in a box, with tissue paper," I said. "I chased him and couldn't catch him. I didn't get a good look at him."

"You got the box?"

"Yeah, and the rose and the paper. I'll bet there's no prints on it."

"I'll bet you're right," Quirk said. "But we'll try. Can you bring it over?"

"No," I said. "I'm not leaving her alone."

"May be just one of the fruitcakes she treats," Quirk said.

"Still not leaving her alone," I said.

"Yeah. Okay, I'll send somebody over. If it's one of her fruitcakes, there might be prints."

I hung up and sipped my second cup. Instant coffee has much less caffeine than ground coffee; two cups of instant was practically none. I put the water on to heat for a third cup.

Susan's phone rang. It was separate from the office phone. I picked it up and said, "Hello."

Hawk's voice said, "Susan?"

I said, "Nobody likes a minority smart-ass."

"True," Hawk said. "What you need?"

I told him about the rose intruder.

Hawk said, "And he punched you in the head and you chased him and he got away? Was he a brother?"

"I don't think so," I said.

"You let a white guy run away from you?"

"What do you want from me," I said. "I'm a white guy too."

"Yeah, you so funky sometimes I forget. I'll come over in case we have to chase him again."

At two minutes to eight Susan appeared wearing a salt-and-pepper-tweed jacket over a black turtleneck. She had on a full black skirt and black shoes with a short heel.

"You are more beautiful than a bird dog on point," I said.

"And damned near as smart," Susan said. "I know we have to talk more. But I simply can't right now. I know you can't leave me unprotected, but I cannot have you or

Hawk lounging in my waiting room when the patients come."

"I'm going to get your front door fixed and then one of us will be around, but we won't be in the way and we won't scare the patients."

"Yes," she said. She kissed me. I patted her on the fanny and she was out and down to her office as her first patient arrived. I heard her say "Come along" as I stood at the top of the stairs out of sight.

12

A carpenter named Shutt came over and replaced Susan's jimmied front door. I gave Susan my S&W .32 to keep in her desk drawer, and Hawk and I took turns lingering at the top of Susan's stairs while she conducted business. There are few things more boring than standing around at the top of a stairwell out of sight.

When Susan got through that night I took her down to Cambridge Police Headquarters to get her a pistol permit. The gun guy was a bear-shaped Tac cop who'd served two tours in Vietnam and did some gunsmithing on the side.

"Can she shoot?" he said.

"Taught her myself," I said.

"I was afraid of that." The cop's name was Steve Costa. "Let's go up to the range, ma'am. Have you fire some rounds to qualify."

"What if I don't qualify?" Susan said.

Costa grinned. "You'll qualify," he said.

We went upstairs and along a corridor lined with tired yellow tiles. Costa unlocked the door and we went into the range.

"Lovely," Susan said.

"Yeah, they don't waste much time on the range," Costa said.

The room looked like an afterthought, jammed into a forgotten space under a long stairwell. There was a small shooting table on which a coffee can full of brass had tipped over and spilled most of the cartridge casings on the floor. Costa walked down the narrow alley of the range and pinned a target onto the trolley with a clothespin. He set the target about fifteen feet away and walked back to the shooting table.

"As you can see, ma'am, the target consists of the silhouette of a man surrounded by increasingly concentric circles; the smallest circle, around the man's head and heart area, is worth ten points. The next circle is worth nine, and so on until the last circle, outside of which there is no score."

"Please call me Susan."

"Okay, Susan. In order to qualify for a license to carry firearms you have to score seventy, firing a maximum of thirty rounds."

"Fine," Susan said.

"Want to fire some for practice, Susan?"

"No, thank you."

I took the thirty-two out and laid it, pointing downrange, on the table beside her. We put on the earmuffs.

Costa said, " 'Cause Spenser and I go way back, I'm going to give you a little head start."

He took out his own gun, a nickel-plated .38 with a black rubber grip, settled into a two-hand shooting crouch, and put six shots inside the 10 circle. He and Susan walked down to look at the target.

"Why, I seem to be within ten points of qualifying already," she said. Her smile was full of innocent amazement. Costa reloaded his gun.

"Here," he said, "use this one. It's all sighted in." It also shot the same size rounds as the bullet holes in the target. Susan caught on at once.

"Sure," she said. She picked up the gun, held it carefully in both hands, stood as I'd taught her to, cocked the gun with her right thumb, fired carefully, six shots, single action, and put all six inside the 7 circle. Then she put the thirty-eight back down on the shooter's table and waited while Costa went down to get the target.

"You forgot to yell, 'Freeze, dirt bag,' " I said.

"Couldn't I say something else, like 'It's all right, I'm a doctor'?" she said.

I shook my head in disgust. "Don't you watch television?" I said.

Costa came back with the target and said, "That's good shooting, Susan. You've qualified, no problem. Want to fire a few rounds just to get the feel of your weapon?"

Susan said, "No, thank you."

Costa turned to me. "Six rounds each?" he said. "For a case of beer?"

"Double action," I said. "Ten seconds to get all the shots off."

"Sure," Costa said, and picked up his gun, reloaded, and put six rounds into the new target in eight seconds. He dumped the brass, reloaded, put the gun on his hip, and went down to collect his target and hang a new one. I took my place, got out the Python, and when Costa said "Go," I fired six rounds in seven seconds.

We both had all our shots in the kill zone, but Costa had four bull's-eyes and I had two.

"Budweiser," Costa said.

"Budweiser?"

"That's right," Costa said. "I drive a Chevy too."

"The heartbeat of America," I said. "I'll drop it off tomorrow."

As we left, Costa said, "Nice shooting, Susan. We'll expedite that permit; should have it by the time the beer arrives."

Walking to the car, Susan said, "I thought you were a good shot."

"I am a good shot," I said, "but Costa shoots every day."

Susan nodded. "I could have qualified without help, but I didn't want to take away his nice gesture."

"You always get it," I said.

"Now, let's go and get a cup of coffee and some cheesecake and decide what we think about the Red Rose business."

We drove over to Chelsea to sit at a Formica table in the Washington Deli. I had some cherry cheesecake and, in utter abandon, a cup of fresh-brewed coffee. Susan had decaff and plain cheesecake. I took a bite of mine and swallowed it, followed by a small sip of coffee, black.

"Ah, wilderness," I said.

"Isn't that supposed to involve a loaf of bread and a jug of wine?"

"And thou, sweets, don't forget thou."

She had a small bite of cheesecake, edging a narrow sliver off one corner of the wedge with her fork.

"The Red Rose killer should not be in therapy," Susan said. "The killings should be the relief he needs from pressure."

"I know," I said. "You said that. But that was before some guy went to a lot of trouble to put a red rose in your front hall."

"It doesn't mean one of my patients is the killer," Susan said.

"It means something," I said. "And it means something worrisome."

"Yes," Susan said. "I agree with that."

"The guy that left it either is or is not one of your patients," I said. "Let's assume he is. Assuming he isn't asks for several more farfetched hypotheses than the assumption that he is."

"I don't like to think it," Susan said.

"So what?" I said.

She smiled. "Yes, of course. Is there anything either of us knows better than the uselessness of deciding what you want to think." She took another nearly transparent sliver from her cheesecake and a sip of coffee.

"It is work where one encounters atypical people," she said. "Some of them can be frightening. If one is to do the work, one puts the fear aside."

"I know," I said.

"Yes." She smiled and put her hand on top of mine. "You would surely know about that."

My cheesecake was gone, and the cherries only a memory in my mouth. I finished my coffee.

"The bond of trust between therapist and patient is the fundament of the therapy. I cannot conspire, even with you, to identify and track any of them."

"If it is Red Rose," I said, "it's not just you that's at risk."

"I'm not sure I'm at risk at all," Susan said. "It is unlikely that he would change the object of his need suddenly to a white psychotherapist."

"It doesn't have to be sudden. Its manifestation would seem sudden, but he may have been changing slowly in therapy for the last year," I said.

Susan shrugged.

"And," I said, "you have explained to me how people like Red Rose are working with a private set of symbols. You may fit that symbolic scheme in some way, just as the black women did."

"Possibly," Susan said, "but it is still highly unlikely that a serial murderer would be in psychotherapy. People come to therapy when the pressure of their conflicting needs gets unbearable."

"Maybe the psychotherapy is part of the need," I said. "Maybe he needs the opportunity to talk about it."

"But he hasn't. I have no clients talking of serial murders."

"Maybe he's still talking about them so symbolically that you don't know it," I said. "Can a patient fool you?"

"Certainly," Susan said. "Obviously it's not in his or her best interest to do so."

"He obviously has a need to be caught," I said. "The letter to Quirk, the tape to me."

"The tape to you may not be like the letter to Quirk," Susan said.

"Maybe not, but that makes it more likely that he's connected to you," I said. "Jealousy, or some such."

Susan made a noncommittal nod.

"Jack," I said to the counterman, "I need more coffee."

"Ted does the coffee," Jack said. "I do the celery tonic."

Ted poured some coffee and brought it out and set it down in front of me.

"Planning to stay up all night?" he said.

"Caution to the winds," I said. I put some cream in and some sugar. I had a theory about diluting the caffeine. Ted went back behind the counter.

"And," I said to Susan, "the red rose in your house. It almost got him caught."

"If it was he," Susan said.

"Coming to you might be part of the desire to get caught," I said.

"Or noticed," Susan said.

"And maybe if he gets too close to getting caught, or noticed," I said, "he'll want to save himself by killing you."

Susan was looking at the paintings on the walls.

"This is the only deli I've ever been to that had art on the walls," she said.

I didn't say anything.

"It's possible," Susan said. She was looking full at me now and I could feel the weight of her will. "But I cannot act on the possibility. I need much more."

I looked back at her without comment. My chin was resting on top of my folded hands. Sigmund Spenser.

"I will," Susan said, "keep the gun in my desk drawer, and I will keep it on my bedside table at night." She pursed her lips a little bit and relaxed them. "And I will use it if I have to."

"Okay," I said. "I know you will. And I'm going to try and find out which one of your patients it is, and I won't tell you how I'm going to do it, because I don't know what will compromise your work and what won't."

Susan laughed without very much pleasure. "It's hard to say whether we're allies or adversaries in this," she said.

"We're allies in everything, pumpkin," I said. "It's just that we don't always go about it like other people."

"Good point," Susan said, and picked up her cup of cold coffee and drank it just as if it were hot.

13

I was in Susan's kitchen cleaning up breakfast when the phone rang. It was Quirk.

"Washburn's confessed," he said.

"Not surprising," I said.

"He confessed to being the Red Rose killer," Quirk said.

I didn't say anything for a minute.

"Yeah," Quirk said, "me too."

"It's bullshit," I said.

"I think he did his wife," Quirk said. "I don't believe the rest."

"What's the chain of command think?"

"Chain of command is so happy to have an arrest, they'd buy Daisy Duck for it if they had a confession," Quirk said.

"What about the guy that left the rose with Susan?" I said.

"Nobody cares about him, they don't want to hear about him," Quirk said. "You're sticking close?"

"For the moment," I said. "Hawk's coming by around ten."

"When he gets there, come over to my office," Quirk said.

I put the dishes in the dishwasher and wiped off the counter and sat to read the *Globe*. They didn't have it yet. But they would. The TV people would get it first probably, but everyone would have it soon and another ring would be added to the circus.

Hawk strolled in at 9:59. He was always on time. In fact he always did everything he said he'd do. He was carrying a gym bag.

"Cops got a confession," I said.

Hawk put the gym bag on the counter in the kitchen.

"Quirk like it?" Hawk said.

"No," I said.

"Tell him about the guy ran away from you the other night?"

"Yeah."

"How Susan going to deal with it?"

"She's got a thirty-two in the desk drawer and you or me sitting around up here."

"No names?"

"No."

Hawk nodded. He opened his gym bag and took out some audio tapes, a paperback copy of *Common Ground*, and a copy of *Ring* magazine. He put the tapes in a neat pile beside Susan's stereo, put *Common Ground* on the coffee table next to the couch, took his gun out of the shoulder holster and placed it beside *Common Ground,* and settled back on the couch with *Ring.*

"You going to see Quirk?" he said.

"Yeah. You know where everything is?"

"Un huh."

It was one of those deceptive days in April when it seems like spring and the wind is a velvet conceit on the lingering reality of winter. I parked on Berkeley Street by a sign that said POLICE VEHICLES ONLY and went up to Quirk's office. Belson was there.

"Washburn has it all about right," Quirk said when I sat down. "The rope's a little different. Always before it was cotton. This time it's that plastic stuff you have to melt the ends when you cut it. But the tape's the same, the way she's tied is the same. She was shot the same way. But there's no semen."

"Same gun?"

"No. Same caliber, but not the same gun."

"It was all in the papers," Belson said. "I checked, everything—tape, way the rope was wound, caliber gun, how she was shot, all of it. Anyone could know."

"You do the questioning?" I said to Quirk.

"Me and Frank and twenty others. It's hard to conduct a good interrogation in a case like this."

I nodded. "Everybody that outranks you has to get in on it and maybe claim he broke the case."

"Place was like a fucking cake sale," Belson said. "The fucking commissioner was there, a guy from the mayor's office."

"They told him what to say," I said.

"Sure," Belson said. He took his cigar out of his mouth

and looked at it for a moment and threw it hard into the wastebasket.

"What about the rope being wrong, and the gun being different, and no semen?"

Quirk grinned. "Guy from the mayor's office says it proves he's the one. Says if he was a copycat he'd have got it right. Says because it was his wife he couldn't ejaculate."

"The gun too?"

"Says he probably got rid of it to cover himself and got another one," Quirk said.

"Can't be a dope and work in the mayor's office," I said. "What about Washburn?"

"Managed a hamburger joint over on Huntington Ave. No connection with the cops, no record of a registered gun except the murder weapon. No previous record, except one DWI."

"What did he do with the previous gun?" I said.

"Took a cruise on the Jazz Boat, dropped it over the middle of the harbor."

"He know you?"

Quirk shook his head. "Nope. Says he looked up my address after he saw my name in the paper, but he forgot it."

"Why'd he claim to be a cop?"

"Wanted to confuse us," Belson said.

We were quiet in the room. There was an elongated rectangle of sun sprawling across Quirk's nearly empty desk. On the desk was a picture of Quirk's wife, three children, and dog. There was a desk clock that told you the time all over the world. It was never clear why Quirk

81

wanted to know. Quirk was leaning back in his swivel chair, sucking on his lower lip.

"Susan doesn't say absolutely that her guy can't be the guy, does she?" Belson said.

"Shrinks don't say absolutely anything," I said.

"She think he'll come back?"

"Shrinks don't know what people are going to do. They only know why they did it," I said.

"Like cops," Quirk said.

"Except they don't usually know why they did it," I said.

"True," Quirk said. He picked up the picture of his dog from his desk and placed it half an inch closer to the pictures of his children. The rhomboid of sun across his desktop had shifted slightly toward me.

"We've got to know about this guy that left the rose for Susan," Quirk said.

"Yes," I said.

"Washburn was into his second aria for the brass when this guy dropped the rose," Belson said.

"So if he is Red Rose, who the hell is this guy?" Quirk said.

"And if Washburn isn't Red Rose," Belson said.

"Yes," I said.

The three of us sat quietly looking at nothing.

"It isn't Washburn," Quirk said.

I looked at Belson.

"Washburn did his wife," Belson said. "He didn't do the rest."

"Maybe," I said.

"Probably," Quirk said.

"It ain't Washburn," Belson said.

"Hawk with Susan?" Quirk said.

"Yeah."

"Good."

14

Washburn was famous by morning. His name was on the lips of Jane Pauley and his face was on the front page of everyone's morning paper. The mayor was on CNN congratulating the police commissioner, and the police commissioner was generously crediting hard work by the entire department. Six paragraphs into the front page story in the *Globe* was an allusion to Police Lieutenant Martin Quirk, the homicide commander, who expressed some reservations. In paragraph ten it was mentioned that a Boston private detective who had been working on the case with the police was unavailable for comment.

"I'm available," I said.

Susan was eating a piece of whole-wheat toast across her breakfast counter from me.

"Certainly to me," she said.

"Paper says I'm unavailable for comment," I said.

"They probably tried your office and you weren't there," she said.

"Lying bastards," I said.

"Well, aren't we surly this morning," Susan said.

"Everybody's got it solved," I said.

She had another bite of toast. I drank my coffee. Susan's hair was in curlers, her face was devoid of makeup. She wore white silk pajamas with a ruffle, and sleeping had wrinkled them. I stared at her.

"What's the matter?" she said when she caught me.

"I was just wondering why you still look beautiful," I said. "It must not be the makeup and the clothes. It must be you."

She smiled. "Are you drinking at this hour of the morning?"

"You go to my head," I said, "like a sip of sparkling burgundy brew."

"I'm not going to do that," she said, "until after work."

I gnawed on my bagel. She looked at her watch. Susan was always running a little late. There seemed time to finish her toast.

"Any hints from your patients?" I said.

"No."

"If you knew who left the rose and were pretty sure he was Red Rose, would you share?"

"Red Rose has confessed," she said.

"Don't dodge the question."

She nodded, and bit the corner of her toast triangle.

"I guess I would," she said. "But I would have to be sure and it would be . . ." She shook her head and didn't finish the sentence. She tried a new one.

"I came late to this work," she said. "And the work, and my skill at it, makes me possible. It makes us possible, because I am more than the apple of your eye, however glad I am about being that too. I am valuable without you."

"True," I said. There was a bowl of Santa Rosa plums on the counter. I took one and polished it against my pants leg.

"I am rigidly defensive about it," she said.

I bit into the plum.

"To have my autonomy violated by the Red Rose business is nearly intolerable," she said. "And to have you or Hawk here watching over me"—her face tightened as she said it— "is very bitter."

"None of this is your fault," I said.

"Nor yours," she said. "But you must understand that it is like letting you into something that is mine. It is like giving away part of me, to have you question me about my patients."

"I don't want him to kill you," I said.

"I know," she said. "I don't want him to either. And I am less frightened with you here, or Hawk. But you must see that being frightened unless you're here, in the practice of my profession, is a terrible condition to be in for me."

"I know," I said.

"I know you know," Susan said. She smiled her big wide brilliant smile, the one that made you feel like life's focus. "I'm just kvetching."

"Neither Quirk nor Belson believes the confession," I said.

"It exonerates the police," Susan said. "Washburn, according to the news, isn't a cop."

"Yeah, and it gives them a black criminal, which shuts up all the talk about racism, and it keeps the general public from screaming for an arrest. There's a lot of reasons to believe him."

"Except?"

"Except the gun is wrong and the rope is wrong and there's no semen and he's black, so how come he kept finding his victims in places a white guy would find them and how come he took this long to get to his wife?"

"I could speculate on the wife part," Susan said.

"Sure," I said. "But the fact remains that there's a lot of holes, and two very experienced homicide investigators don't believe him."

"A man like Washburn might in fact kill his wife and be so overcome at the guilt of it that he would do this," Susan said.

"Confess to a whole series of crimes?" I said.

"More. He might emulate the criminal in the crime, become him, in a manner of speaking. It would be a way of dramatizing how horrible a crime he was contemplating, and it would, maybe, distance him from it enough so that he could carry it out."

"So his grief and all would be genuine," I said.

"Absolutely. He's done something more horrible than any of his questioners can imagine. Of course he's overcome. And he must be punished on a scale equal to the horribleness. He must not only be a murderer, he must be a fiend, as it were, a noted serial killer."

"So you don't believe his confession either," I said.

"I neither believe nor disbelieve. I could make a scenario for belief too. I'm only trying to give you possibilities in an area I know," Susan said. "If you decide finally that he's innocent or guilty, I will believe you," she said. "I know what I know, and I know what you know. In this you know more."

I finished my plum, and got up and walked around the counter to the other side and gave her a kiss on the mouth.

"Thank you," I said.

"You're welcome."

She looked at her watch.

"Jesus Christ," she said. "I have twenty minutes until my first appointment."

"Try not to trample me," I said, and got out of the way.

15

Quirk called me while Susan was speeding around the apartment.

"Hawk coming over?" he said.

"Yes, at ten."

"Stay there with him. Belson and I are coming by," Quirk said.

"Sure," I said.

As I was hanging up, Susan stopped momentarily in front of me, gave me a kiss on the mouth, and sped to the front door. She looked like a fast sunrise.

"Beep beep," I said.

"I'll call you later," she said, and was gone.

Hawk arrived at ten, Quirk and Belson right behind him.

Hawk said, "This a coincidence, or are you guys after me?"

Quirk shook his head and closed the door behind him and said, "We need help."

Hawk's face broke into a wide smile. "Y'all finally facing up to that," he said.

Belson rummaged around the kitchen until he found a saucer that would serve as an ashtray. Quirk went into the kitchen behind him and carefully shook the water from his raincoat onto the tile floor. Then he hung it from a rack Susan had by the back porch door. Belson started back into the living room with his ashtray.

"Frank," Quirk said, and nodded at the coat.

Belson said, "Yeah," and came back into the kitchen and hung his raincoat up beside Quirk's. Hawk draped his leather jacket over the back of a kitchen chair. Without the jacket the ivory butt of his gun glared at us from under his arm. He wore extra rounds in a pocket on the back of his belt.

Belson glanced around the apartment with its careful clutter of objets d'art, lace, silk, crystal, and velvet. There was a huge crimson fan spread on one wall of the den.

"It's you," Belson said to me.

"Yeah," I said. "I'm looking to buy a paisley gun."

Quirk said, "Belson and I are on vacation."

The cold spring rain was sharp and insistent on the front windows.

"Perfect weather for it," I said.

"Commissioner insisted," Quirk said.

"I noticed in the paper you were expressing reservations," I said.

"Yeah, I did it again on Jimmy Winston's show last night," Quirk said.

"Mobilizing public opinion," Hawk murmured.

"Something," Quirk said. "Anyway, this morning I got put on vacation status, extended. Frank joined me. Some kind of gesture, I guess."

"I been working hard, boss, you know that," Belson said.

Quirk nodded.

"So they are committed to Washburn," I said.

"Yeah," Quirk said.

"Means they figure his story will hold up," Hawk said.

"He's pretty steady on that," Quirk said.

"It's the only thing he is steady on," Belson said. "Everything else, he's only got one oar in the water."

"He'd have to be," I said. I told them Susan's hypothesis.

"It's the only way he can think about what he did," Hawk said. "He probably won't slide on it."

Belson looked at Hawk, and shook his head.

"Whatever his reasons," Quirk said, "I agree he won't waffle on the confession."

"So," I said. "If the real Red Rose is smart, he'll stop killing people for a while and walk away from this without anybody laying a glove on him."

Quirk nodded.

"If he can," Hawk said.

"If he can," Quirk said, "and he's a cop; he can be working in my department, talking with me every day for all I know."

"And if he can't, then he'll kill some more women," I said.

We were quiet. Belson knocked some of the accumulated ash of his cigar into Susan's bright red saucer that matched the bright red fan on the wall, that picked up one of the colors in her Oriental rug, that reflected in its design the shape of the mirror in the hall, that balanced the architectural detail over the archway to the bedroom. The ash didn't match anything.

"We need to find out about this guy left the rose for Susan," Quirk said.

"I been giving that some thought," I said.

"You have a plan?" Quirk said.

"Yeah, we got to do this right," I said. "But the thing to do is stake out Susan's office and identify every one of her patients who could have been the guy I chased."

"Susan won't cooperate?" Belson said.

"No," I said.

"Even to save her own ass?" Belson said.

"Life," I said.

"Yeah, sorry."

"No."

"Doesn't make sense," Belson said.

"To you," Hawk said. "Make sense to Susan."

Belson looked at Hawk again, held the look for a moment, then nodded.

"How long will it take?" Quirk said.

"Should be a week or so; most patients come once or twice a week," I said. "It's the best I can think of."

Quirk nodded.

"Got to be careful," I said. "Some patient leaves psychotherapy and finds a cop following . . ."

"I know," Quirk said. "We can't fuck these people up."

"Susan catch us and we got trouble," Hawk said.

"I know that too," Quirk said.

"Okay," I said. "We watch. First patient arrives at nine and the last patient leaves at six. If they drive, we can get the license numbers. If they walk, we can follow them."

"And one of us is always here with Susan," Quirk said.

"Yeah."

"Can you see from here?" Quirk said. He walked to the window.

"Not well enough. We have to be outside."

Hawk looked out the window. It was dark and the rain was steady.

"Outside the place to be," he said, "on your vacation."

*. . . They thought it was somebody else. A schwartze.
Some wife killer who'd faked it and made it look like he'd
done them all. Talk about lucky. All he had to do was stop
and they'd fry the schwartze and he'd be safe. Could he
stop? Jesus, would he miss it. What a loss. What a hole in
his life. It was what he did. The planning, the stalking,
the catching, the escaping, it organized him. Who was he
without it? What should he do? If he could talk with her
about it? But if she knew, she'd tell. He couldn't see her
anymore. But he wanted her to know.*

"Come in," she said.

*The rain sheeted down along the window behind the
tropical fish tank. The fish seemed restless. Water and
water. He sat in his usual seat. He felt full of his need for
her to know. But she'd tell. He knew she'd tell her boyfriend.*

"When I was little, I was very close to my mother," he
said. She nodded.

"I could tell her anything. 'It's all right,' she'd say, 'I'm
your mother.' "

*She made a tiny rolling motion with her forefinger to
encourage him on.*

"I told her everything."

*She had on a brown glen plaid suit today, with a white
blouse.*

"I remember when I was a little kid, maybe third grade, I, ah, messed my pants."

She nodded; no reaction, no disgust, no amusement. He could still feel the hot embarrassment of it.

"They called my mother and she came and got me and she was nice about it and said it could happen to anyone. And I got to go home with her and I asked her not to tell and she promised she wouldn't . . .

"One of her friends was there, and when I came downstairs from taking a bath the friend teased me about it."

"So she had told," she said.

He nodded. "I . . ." He stopped and swallowed. He seemed unable to speak.

"You couldn't trust her," she said.

Again he could only nod. It was like his voice was paralyzed. He could breathe okay and swallow okay, but he seemed like he couldn't talk. The silence seemed heavy. The rain chattered against the window behind her. No fish in this room. Just the waiting room. He breathed through his mouth.

She waited.

"I never said anything," he finally said. His voice sounded reedy and nearly detached from him.

"If you had?"

"She'd have got mad. She never admitted she was wrong. She just got mad at me if I said anything."

"What happened when she got mad?"

"She didn't love me."

She nodded.

"What kind of love is that?" his voice said. "What kind

is it when you can love me and not love me whenever you feel like it?"

She shook her head gently, and again it was quiet except for the rain.

16

Hawk took the day shift with Susan. Belson and I went outside with Quirk and sat in his car. Me and Quirk in front, Belson in the back seat. The rain streaked the windows, blurring everything. "No wipers," I said. "Three guys sitting in a car with the motor running and the wipers on is like putting a flashing blue light on the roof."

"Can you see well enough to identify anyone?" Quirk said.

We were across the street and half a block up from Susan's house.

"No," I said. "But we're not making fine discriminations here. Any white male who looks like he could outrun me."

Quirk nodded. "Frank," he said, "you want to take the first one?"

"Sure."

We were quiet. The rain stayed with us. After ten minutes the windows started to fog and Quirk cracked the windows on the side away from Susan's office. At ten of eleven a patient came out of Susan's front door and down the steps.

"How about him?" Quirk said.

"He's the right size," I said. The outlines of the man were blurred and soft through the wet window. "He white?"

"If he's not," Belson said, "I'll drop him." He got out of the back seat on the sidewalk side and began walking up Linnaean Street toward Garden, parallel with Susan's patient on the other side of the street.

After a moment Quirk said to me, "Okay, he's the right color."

"Now if Belson doesn't lose him," I said.

"Belson won't lose him," Quirk said. "And the guy won't make him."

I nodded. "And if he gets in a car, Frank gets the number."

"And we ID him that way," Quirk said. "When's the next one?"

"Should arrive any minute, and come out about ten of twelve."

"The fifty-minute hour," Quirk said.

We watched the rain slide along the windows. At five of eleven a woman in a tan trench coat with a violet kerchief over her head went up the four steps to Susan's front door, rang the bell, and went in.

"Shit," Quirk said.

"Nothing now until ten of one," I said. "Might as well get some coffee."

98

We left the car so we wouldn't lose the spot and walked up Linnaean to Mass. Ave. and had coffee in a bakery. Also a bagel each. With cream cheese. By twelve-thirty we were back in the car waiting. At six minutes to one a woman in a belted red raincoat came out and opened a black umbrella on Susan's porch. Quirk and I said nothing.

"If there's many that fit the requirements," Quirk said, "this will take a while. We could use more manpower."

"Not Hawk," I said. "He stays where he is."

Quirk nodded. "I can't use any of my people."

"Unofficially?" I said. "Sort of a favor?"

Quirk shook his head. "It would cost them. I'm excommunicated, until I agree with the official version."

"You and Galileo," I said.

"Didn't he throw his balls off the leaning tower?" Quirk said.

"That too," I said.

At two minutes of one a burly man wearing a fingertip-length black leather jacket and a Totes crush rain hat went into Susan's office.

"Charley Mahoney," Quirk said. "Vice."

"Nope," I said. "Too heavy. I could catch him in half a block."

"When you do, you better be ready," Quirk said.

We lapsed into silence again. The next two clients were women. At two minutes past four a man with an open golf umbrella turned into Susan's front walk and up the steps.

"Could be him," I said.

"Late too," Quirk said. "I'll take him when he comes out."

At 4:53 the guy came out, opened his umbrella, and

headed back down Linnaean Street toward Mass. Ave. with Quirk behind him.

At 4:56 a middle-sized tallish guy came along wearing a khaki bush jacket and one of those Australian campaign hats with one side of the brim tied up against the crown. I didn't suspect him of being an Aussie soldier. This was Cambridge.

He came out of Susan's at three minutes to six and started down Linnaean Street toward Mass. Ave. He was on the left side of the street. I got out and headed down the right side, maybe three car lengths back of him. It was still raining and it was beginning to get darker. I studied his walk through the rain, trying to catch a familiar movement. But walking and running are different movements. He was the right size and he had an easy athletic walk. The rain was coming down as if it planned on staying forever. I had on jeans, white leather Reeboks, a gray T-shirt, a leather jacket, and a felt hat that Paul Giacomin had bought me, which looked like you would wear it in Kenya if you were Stewart Granger. The Reeboks were wet through quickly, but the rest stood up to the rain pretty well. Tailing him was easy because he hunched into the rain with his head down and, except when he crossed Linnaean in front of me to head down Mass. Ave. toward Harvard Square, I didn't have to do anything very wily.

If a guy doesn't know he's being tailed, or doesn't care, tailing is not brain surgery. Mostly it takes a little concentration not to get caught staring at your man in the reflection from a store window, or getting too far behind so that if he gets on a subway, or a bus, you're left standing. Ideally you have a backup so that the tail keeps changing, and you have somebody in a car in case the guy has one or grabs a cab. I've yet to find a cabbie that responds when you say "Follow that cab." The last guy I tried slammed on the brakes and slapped down his meter and told me to take a walk. "I look like fucking James Bond to you?" he said.

On the right, Cambridge Common was soggy and unattended. The only movement was a kid in a plaid skirt and a yellow hip-length slicker, walking a big black Lab wearing a red kerchief for a collar. The kid had no hat on and her long black hair was plastered to her scalp and neck. The dog sniffed rapidly in a large circle around the base of the war memorial statue and then lay down on his side in a large puddle, his feet straight out before him, his tongue lolling.

"Othello, you asshole," the kid said.

At Harvard Square, Mass. Ave. turns off east toward Boston. Brattle Street heads west toward Watertown, and John F. Kennedy Street goes on down to the river. In the distorted triangle formed at this point is the famed out-of-town newsstand, and the Harvard Square subway entrances. A couple of small round kiosks that look vaguely Byzantine dispense information and theater tickets. The kids who drifted in tattered clusters in and around the triangle were mostly scrawny and pale and very young. They wore silly clothes and ludicrous haircuts and listened to tiring music on portable radios. Occasionally there was a guitar, a kind of nod toward tradition, which for them was the sixties. They were there, perhaps, because they had nowhere else to be, even in the cold spring rain, sheltered beneath the subway entrance, struggling to look aloof from middle-class values.

My man stopped under the roof of the subway entrance and looked at a group of five punkers across the entrance from him. A thin kid with skinny white arms left the others and came out and spoke with my man. The kid wore a short-sleeved leather jacket over his narrow bare chest. He had on black tights, probably made from polyester, tucked inside black motorcycle boots. The jacket and the boots were both studded with silver. The kid's hair was pink and cut in a high mohawk and he had maybe nine silver earrings in one ear. Bravado.

My man nodded and stepped out into the rain, and the kid went with him. They continued up Mass. Ave. together in the rain. The kid's Mohawk wilted a little, but didn't run. Even in the rain there was a lot of street activity. People coming home from work, students going to the library, or the barroom, or the movies, a scattering of tourists coming to see the famous Harvard Square and looking vaguely puzzled when they found it. On the north side of Mass. Ave., Harvard did its red brick loom, while on the south side the Holyoke Center, which was also Harvard, seemed grayer than usual in the wet evening.

At Putnam Street, where Mount Auburn merges with Mass. Ave., we three turned toward the river, past the big furniture store and into a sort of shabby neighborhood where there wasn't much foot traffic. I dropped farther back. It was getting tricky now. Most of the homes here were multiple dwellings, and if he turned into one, I might end up with a choice of six names. I closed up. My man stopped before a green two-story, and gave a quick glance about. Furtive, since he'd joined the kid.

I walked past them, my head ducked into the rain that seemed to be coming straight up Putnam Street off the river. A few steps beyond, I stopped and looked in the window of an Italian delicatessen and watched them by turning my eyes while I kept my head straight. My man watched me for a moment. The boy shook his arm and said something, and my man nodded and headed in the walk along the side of the building.

I waited a full minute and walked back up Putnam Street. There was no one in sight. I turned in the same walkway that my man had taken and there was a side entrance. It was closed. As I stopped in front of it a light went on above me on the second floor. I bent close and looked at the nameplate. It was not dark yet, but it had gotten murky and I couldn't read it. There was no one else in sight. I reached inside my leather jacket and took out a pair of twelve-dollar magnifiers and put them on and looked again. The nameplate said PHILIP ISELIN, PH.D. If it had been sunny, I could have read it without glasses.

17

When I got back from following Philip Iselin, Hawk and Susan were standing in her waiting room on the first floor, looking at the fish tank. The tank hood was off, there was something that looked like oil slick on the surface of the water and in the oil slick floated a red rose. In various stages of suspension in the water beneath the surface, the tropical fish floated dead, or in two instances dying.

"Probably gasoline," Hawk said. "Smells like it."

I nodded, looking at Susan. The filter apparatus in the fish tank continued to bubble pointlessly, easily over-matched by the gasoline.

"I don't know when it happened," Susan said. "The front door is unlocked during the day, obviously, and any-one could walk in while I was with a patient."

"No way to hear him?" I said.

"No. Patients normally ring the bell and walk into the

waiting room. There is a double door system to my office to ensure privacy."

Hawk looked over at the office doors. There were two of them. One opened out, into the waiting room; the other opened into the office. Privileged information.

"But it would require a patient to know the routine," I said.

"Most therapists probably have a not dissimilar routine," Susan said.

"Aw, come on, Susan," Hawk said. "If it not one of your patients we got to imagine somebody walking around with gasoline in his pocket and a red rose, looking for working fish tank."

"And being lucky enough," I said, "to wander in here by accident and find one."

Susan nodded.

"Wishful thinking," she said. "But it doesn't mean he or she is the Red Rose killer."

"*She* is wishful thinking too," I said. "Unless you want to believe that this is a different person than the one who broke in here the other night and left a rose."

Susan took in a long, slow breath.

"That would be asking a lot of coincidence," she said. "So it's probably a *he,* and it's probably one of my patients. But it doesn't have to be probably the killer."

"But we can't act as if it weren't," I said. "Can we get a list of your patients today?"

She shook her head.

"God, you're stubborn," I said.

"Yes, but it's more than that," Susan said. "It seems to me that anyone planning to do this would do so on a day he wasn't scheduled. And it seems to me that it is someone trying to say something to me that he can't yet say in therapy. If it is the killer, our best hope may be to keep him in therapy until he tells me he's the one. If it is not the killer, the reasons to keep him anonymous must be obvious."

I looked at Hawk. He shrugged very slightly. "Smart too," he said.

"If the Red Rose killer does, in fact, surface in therapy, could you take the time to mention it to one of us," I said.

"Oh, don't be so pissy," Susan said. "You know I will when I'm sure. I don't want anyone else killed, including me."

"Pissy?" I said.

"Pissy," Susan said. "I shouldn't expect you to understand all the technical terms of my profession."

"You want to clean out the tank?" I said.

"Yes," Susan said. "And I want to put more fish in."

"Don't disturb the patients?"

"No, in fact I wish to disturb one. I wish to thwart and frustrate whoever poisoned the fish. It will force him to rechannel whatever he's trying to express, and perhaps he'll rechannel it my way."

"You shrinks are a devious bunch," I said. "What if he rechannels it violently?"

Susan smiled sweetly.

"Why, then you or Hawkie-poo will intervene," she said. "Why else are you hanging around?"

I had nothing to say to that. Neither did Hawkie-poo.

. . . Was she scared? She must be scared. They were all scared when it came down to it. Any woman could be frightened. Had she guessed it was him? Had her boyfriend seen him clearly? The thought that she might know nearly smothered him with its lovely frenzy. Maybe someday . . .

"I saw your name in the paper."

She said, "Um hmm."

Maybe someday . . .

"Your boyfriend's working on the Red Rose case."

"Um hmm."

Maybe someday . . . The fear slivered through him.

"Why would a guy do something like that?"

She merely looked interested. She didn't speak.

The sensation he felt as he talked with her was reminiscent of the way it felt to wiggle a loose tooth when he was small. She suspected him. It was like undressing in front of her. Look at this.

"I'm sort of fascinated with this guy, this Red Rose guy."

"Um hmm?" she said. There was encouragement in her voice, no disapproval.

"You don't mind me talking about it?"

"No," she said. "See what it leads to."

"My mother would have been . . ." He did an imitation

107

of his mother's uncomfortable disapproving frown. "She hated anything dirty."

"What kinds of things did she consider dirty?"

"You know, sex, anything about sex."

She nodded. She understood.

"And your father?" *she said.*

"He loved her so much. He did everything she wanted . . . except stop drinking."

"So she was the power in the family," *she said.*

"No, yes, well, it was funny. We all pretended she was, and we said how smart she was, and how she could always fix things and find things and figure out things. But in fact she was weak and stupid and scared of everything, and it was like a game my father and me played. Except we never said."

"Did you know?" *She sat very quietly, her big eyes on his face. She was very interested and very kind.*

"Not then, except I did. I guess I did and I didn't, does that make sense?"

She nodded her head. "Sure," *she said.*

"I mean, she'd be telling you absolutely how things were and ought to be and you believed her and at the same time you knew she didn't know anything about it. I mean, she couldn't tell you where Brazil was. And she couldn't read very well, and she lived at home until she married my father and lived with him the rest of the time, until he died."

She was sitting a little forward in her chair now, her knees together, her hands in her lap.

"And she was never really interested in either one of us. She said she was, but she never really paid any attention to what you said, or had any sense of what you cared about. I don't think she understood much, and when anyone talked about things it made her scared."

The room was quiet. She sat, wearing a black suit. He thought of her putting on the suit in the morning. He could feel tears at the edge of crying. He was breathing only a little air at a time, small breaths, rapidly.

"But she loved me," he said.

"And if you didn't play the game, she wouldn't," she said.

He couldn't speak. He nodded. They sat quietly together while he struggled with his breathing and his tears.

"Weakness," she said, "can be powerful, can't it?"

He nodded again.

"And frightening."

"Yes," he said. His voice sounded strangled. He wanted to tell her the other thing. The thing he never told. He opened his mouth. He could feel the thing close on him. He couldn't. He never had. He couldn't.

18

In seven days Quirk and Belson and I had gotten up a list of seven suspects. Everyone else was too female, or too old, the wrong color, or the wrong size.

We sat in my office on a lovely bright Saturday morning and drank coffee while Quirk listed the seven possibilities on the blackboard.

"Okay," Quirk said, "here's what we got." His excommunication hadn't made a dent in his lieutenant-ness. "In order we spotted them: The first guy Belson tailed is named Gordon Felton, lives in Charlestown, near Thompson Square. Works as a security guard for an outfit in Boston called Bullet Security Systems, Inc."

Belson grinned. "Probably got crossed Uzis on their calling cards," he said.

"Makes him sort of a cop," I said.

"Sort of," Quirk said. "Your man is Phil Iselin, instructor

in Eastern studies at Harvard, lives where you found him on Putnam Street. Third one is Mark Charles, intern at Boston City Hospital, lives in the South End, West Newton Street. Number four is Lewis Larson, he's a cop, works out of station fifteen in a cruiser. Number five is a guy runs a gourmet food store in Wellesley, Edward Eisner—lives next to the store. Number six is Ted Sparks, teaches math at MIT, lives in Boston on Lime Street. Number seven is a French national named Emil Gagné, who's a graduate student in politics at the Kennedy School and lives in a condo on Mount Auburn Street."

Quirk paused and looked at us. We looked back. So far Quirk was just getting his ducks in a row. There wasn't much cause for excitement. "So one of these seven is probably the guy you chased," Quirk said.

"Been a hell of a lot easier if you'd caught him," Belson said, "or at least got a good look."

"Maybe we should line them up and have them race me," I said. "The ones I beat aren't it."

"Nothing from Susan?" Quirk said.

"Nope. Hawk's been there all day every day with the upstairs door open. There's been no trouble and Susan isn't reporting anything special."

"Hawk enjoying himself?" Belson said.

"Like the birdman of Alcatraz," I said.

Belson smiled. "It's the closest Hawk's ever come to jail," he said.

"Keeps him off the street," Quirk said.

"Now that I've narrowed it for you to seven, do you suppose you could find out which one is Red Rose?" I said. "While you're on sabbatical?"

111

"Are we not trained investigators?" Quirk said.

"Without getting us sued by the Boston Psychoanalytic Institute?" I said.

"Maybe we get fired," Quirk said. "We'll open our own firm. Quirk and Belson, Private Inquiries."

"Always a lieutenant," Belson said. "Alphabetically it should be Belson and Quirk."

"We find anything, we'll be in touch," Quirk said to me.

"Check the security guard and the cop first," I said.

"Yeah," Quirk said.

"Everyone else is what you'd expect to find, even the cop, because of you steering them," I said. "But how many security guards are getting psychotherapy from a Cambridge shrink, do you think?"

"There must be some," Belson said.

"Yeah, but everyone else but the cop fits the pattern, and we can sort of explain the cop—job stress, Susan's reputation, word of mouth among the fuzz. The security guard is the atypical one. You got to start someplace."

Quirk nodded. "I'll let you know what we find," he said.

19

I had the answering machine on in my office while I baby-sat Susan and waited for Quirk and Belson to come up with something. In one of the oddest pairings since Mutt and Jeff, Hawk was helping them, and I was alone with my books and my radio and my Colt Python up in Susan's living room with the door ajar.

I felt isolated and bored and useless and frustrated. My desire for the guy who'd left the rose and outrun me was tangible, like lust, and it tingled along my neck and shoulder muscles all the time I sat and waited and listened.

To pass the time I beeped my answering machine and found a message from a woman named Sara, who said she was a producer for the Jimmy Winston show and would I come on and talk about Red Rose.

I called her.

"Oh," she said, very upbeat, "thanks for calling back.

We know that not everyone is satisfied that this man Washburn is really the Red Rose killer."

I said, "Un huh."

She said, "And we can't get anyone to talk about it. We had the homicide commander on by phone-in last week, but since then no one in the police department or the district attorney's office will even return our calls."

"Happens to me all the time," I said. "Makes you doubt yourself sometimes."

"Ah, yes. Anyway, we know you've been involved in this case, and we wondered if perhaps you could come on some night and talk with Jimmy, and perhaps take some calls."

"Sure," I said. The department couldn't force me to take a vacation.

"Would it be possible," she said, "to come tonight?"

"Sure," I said, "as long as I can bring a date."

"Certainly," Sara said.

Which is how it came about that Susan and I were going up in an elevator in a building near Government Center at quarter to ten at night.

"Why are you doing this, again?" Susan said.

"Sort of getting even for Quirk," I said. "He has to do what he's told. I don't."

"Yes," Susan said. "I've noticed that about you."

The elevator reached the seventh floor and we reported to the female guard at the reception desk. I noticed she was not from Bullet Security. The guard made a call, and in a minute a chunky blond woman wearing maroon harlequin eyeglasses came down the hall.

"Hi," she said. "I'm Sara. Jimmy's waiting for you."

We went down the hall and into the studio where Jimmy Winston, wearing earphones, was listening to a caller. He nodded as we came in and waved me to a seat across the U-shaped console from him. There was a swivel chair and earphones hanging from a nail. On a wall opposite Jimmy were the station's call letters in large print and the call-in phone number in equally large print. Below the numbers was a glass window and through that the control room. I sat in the swivel chair, Susan sat in another, pushed back against the wall by the door. I noticed that Jimmy checked her legs when she sat.

"Well, you're entitled to your opinion," Jimmy said into the mike, "but frankly I'm sick of listening to it."

He made a cut motion at the control room.

"This is WKDK, the *Thought* of Boston, and I'm Jimmy Winston, back after *this* five-minute newsbreak."

He pointed again at the control room. And leaned back in his chair and swiveled toward me. Through the glass I saw a cadaverous-looking newscaster settle in beside the engineer and begin to read the news.

"They're out there howling tonight," Jimmy Winston said. He was a fat guy with a crew cut who wore dark glasses indoors. Black-rimmed Raybans. He had a long-collared white shirt open halfway down his chest. His slacks were some kind of gray worsted, and he had his shoes off under the console.

"You're the detective," he said.

I nodded. "This is Susan Silverman," I said.

He nodded briefly at Susan.

"So whaddya know that you haven't been telling?" he said.

"I've got a recipe for cornmeal pancakes," I said, "that I've never made public."

Jimmy's smile was automatic and meaningless.

"Yeah, great. How about the serial killer? You figure the cops got the wrong guy?"

Sara came into the room and handed Jimmy a piece of typescript.

"We gotta change the promo, Jimmy. And there's a PSA after the promo where you just read the tag, okay?"

"Jesus Christ," Jimmy said. "Why not wait till I'm on the goddamned air to tell me. What genius changed the promo, you?"

"The programming . . ." Sara started.

Jimmy waved his hand.

"Never mind, for chrissake. I haven't got time. Beat it. I'll read this through and fix it on the air."

Sara smiled painfully at us and scurried out. Jimmy shook his head and rolled his eyes at me.

"Dizzy little broad," he said, and turned his attention to the new promo copy. I looked at Susan. She smiled at me serenely. "This is going to be really exciting," Susan said.

The newscaster got through, and Jimmy turned the sound up on the studio speaker. A commercial for a car dealer came on.

"Okay, we got about thirty seconds," Jimmy said. "I'll set the scene by asking you a couple things, then we go to the calls. You'll need the earphones for the calls." He looked sort of like a toad, but his voice had the rich timbre that professional voices have. Full of authority. Brook no insolence. Trust me. The air light went on and Jimmy said,

"This is WKDK, the *Thought* of Boston, and I'm Jimmy Winston. This hour we'll be talking with a Boston private eye who says there's police cover-up in the Red Rose killings and is here to back it up with fact. How'd you first get on this case, Mr. Spenser?"

I was looking at Susan. "Police cover-up," she mouthed silently, and smiled at me as sweetly as a field of alfalfa.

"I was asked on by the man in charge of the investigation."

Jimmy looked at his notes. "That would be Homicide Lieutenant Martin Quirk," he said. Everything he said sounded like either an accusation or the announcement of World War Three.

"Yes."

"He's no longer on the case," Winston said. "Why are you? You think Washburn's innocent?"

"I don't think Washburn is the Red Rose killer," I said. "He looks good for it, and solves everybody's problems if he goes down for it. But I think the genuine article is still walking around loose."

"Even though the top criminal investigative officials in the Commonwealth are convinced otherwise?"

"Daunting," I said. "But yes."

Jimmy lit a cigarette. It was maybe his fifth since I'd been there.

"You want to solve this," Jimmy said.

"I want it solved."

"But wouldn't you rather it be solved by you?"

"So I can make the movie deal and have my picture in *People*?"

"I can't believe you hadn't thought of that," Jimmy said.

"Try," I said.

"You have evidence?" Jimmy said. "If you do, maybe you could tell us what it is, and maybe explain why neither the chief of police nor the Suffolk County District Attorney's office has it."

I gave him everything I had except the stuff about Susan and our gang of seven. Jimmy looked disgusted.

"You haven't got anything Lieutenant Quirk didn't have," he said. "Time for the phones." He looked at the small TV screen in front of him and saw six names displayed along with the towns from which they were calling.

"We've got Clara from Boston. Hi, Clara, you're on the *Thought* of Boston."

"Hi. Jimmy?"

"Go ahead, you're on the air."

"Jimmy, I love your show. I wanted to tell you that."

"Thank you. Do you have a question for our guest?" Jimmy said.

"Yeah. Mr. Spenser?"

"Yes, Clara?"

"You seen the bodies, right?"

"Yes."

"They were all undressed?"

"Yes."

"And raped?" Clara said.

"No, not in the traditional sense."

"Sure they was, he raped them and they ought to castrate the animal is what I say."

"You say that often, do you, Clara?"

"If they cut 'em off, he wouldn't be raping women and tying them up."

Jimmy said, "Thanks, Clara, we'll keep you in mind. We have Ronnie from Reading on the line. Hi, Ronnie, you're on the air."

"Jimmy?"

"Yeah, Ronnie, you're on the air. Go ahead."

"Jimmy, I think this whole thing is a media hype, you know. Incidentally, I love your show."

"Thank you."

"I mean, after all, they're only killing each other, you know. I mean, it's not like they were . . . you know. Let's forget about it. My kids was talking about it in school the other day. What kind of thing is this for kids to be talking about. I say let it die, stop stirring up trouble."

Jimmy said, "You're saying because everybody involved is black it shouldn't interest the rest of us?"

"They're just killing each other," Ronnie said.

"Ronnie, you listening to me, Ronnie?" Jimmy said. "I want you now to go out in the garage and start up your car and suck on the tail pipe." He punched up the next button. More callers' names crawled across the television screen. "Marvin from Quincy, go ahead, you're on the air."

"I think Mr., ah, Spenser there, your guest, is right and I appreciate his courage, you unnerstand? I mean they cover stuff up all the time. All they care, they want to look good in the papers, you know. Most of them got on the force so they could push people around . . ."

119

"I think the Negroes should take care of their own problems . . ."

". . . think your mistake is quite simply attempting human solutions to a problem whose cause is elsewhere. Have you ever considered Beelzebub? . . ."

"These crimes are symbolic of a larger sickness in this country. In a sense, every woman is bound and . . ."

And so it went. At ten-thirty I got a call from a guy who suggested that if I was deranged enough to be on this show, I wasn't likely to be much use solving a series of murders.

"Is this you, Goldman?" I said.

"I admit to nothing," the caller said. But it was Maynard Goldman, and I knew it.

"You saying there's something wrong with this show?" Winston said. I could hear the amusement in Maynard's voice.

"If only we could get it down to *something,*" he said.

Winston made the cut sign to the engineer and Maynard was gone. Susan smiled at me encouragingly.

The last caller before the eleven o'clock newsbreak wanted to know, if I ever caught the Red Rose killer, what I'd do to him.

"Make him come on this show," I said.

Jimmy did the news segue and lit up another cigarette as I hung up my earphones and pushed my chair back.

"No need to crap on the show," Jimmy said. "We're the people's forum here. They got a right to their opinion."

"That's not opinion," I said. "That's pathology. This is a forum for public masturbation."

120

Jimmy shrugged and turned back to look at the opening promo copy. "Nice talking to ya," he said.

"Gee," Susan said, "behind all the glamour and glitter . . ."

She took my hand and we left.

20

Hawk was taking a turn sitting with Susan while I went down to the office to look at my mail and bill a couple of clients. I walked up Berkeley Street with the wind coming off the river behind me and scattering McDonald's wrappers before me as I walked. Susan was all right as long as Hawk or I stayed with her, but it was no way to live, and I knew how much she hated needing someone to guard her.

Inside my office I picked up the mail from the pile on the floor beneath the mail slot and went to my desk and sat down with my feet up to open it. There were several calls flashing on my answering machine, and while I opened mail I turned them on.

The first one said, "Hello, nigger lover. I heard you last night on Jimmy Winston, and I heard you trying to say it was a white man instead of letting the nigger fry like he should. Someone ought to shut your mouth for you." I finished reading through my telephone charges, as I always did, with the fond hope that I would catch the bastards in a mistake. There were five more messages on my machine. All concurred in various elegant ways with the first, except one which was a computerized vacation real estate pitch that made me yearn for the racist threats, and one in which a male voice said softly, "Maybe you're right about Red Rose, maybe he's still out there." I stopped looking at my mail and played that one back again. Then I took out the message tape, put in a spare one, and slipped the Red Rose tape in my jacket pocket.

I finished up on the phone bill, opened a note from Rita Fiore, written on lavender paper and smelling of lilac scent. It said she was just checking in to see how I was and maybe we should have lunch. While I was mulling this the door opened into my office and five guys, who clearly did not represent the League of Women Voters, came in one by one and formed a semicircle around my desk. The last guy in shut the door.

"You guys are in the Kerry Drake fan club," I said, "and you've come by to ask me to your next banquet."

The leader was a weight lifter, obviously. The quartet backing him were all good-sized, although none of them would have scared me alone. The weight lifter had on baggy prewashed jeans and black Reebok coaches' shoes and a sleeveless blue muscle shirt that said Universe Gym across the front. Given the weather outside, he must have been freezing, but how else to scare me with his muscles?

He said, "We want to talk with you, nigger lover."

I said, "Ah, didn't I just hear you on the phone?"

He said, "You're trying to get that nigger off."

I said, "Truth, I am truth's servant, and I don't think he did it."

"Yeah, well we do," he said.

"Persuasive," I said.

"We don't like niggers, and we don't like nigger lovers," the weight lifter said.

I felt my frustration slowly catalyze into anger and the anger begin to build. I'd been wrestling with a phantom for weeks now, and here were live bodies, right before me, asking to wrestle. I held on. Five is a lot.

"Could you make a bicep for me?" I said.

The weight lifter actually made a start before he caught himself. I grinned to let him know I'd seen the start.

"Step out around that desk," the weight lifter said.

"Or you'll come around and get me," I said.

He was in the center, slightly forward of the other four. The guy to his right was red-haired and square-shouldered with a swarm of freckles on his face.

The weight lifter grinned slightly at his pals and said, "Yeah."

I got up from my chair and walked around my desk. Without breaking stride I kicked him in the groin. I put a straight left into his pal's face and pulled my gun from under my arm with my right hand. The other three froze in a kind of tableau.

The weight lifter sank to his knees, hands and forearms pressed between his legs. Red had taken maybe two steps back and was rocking back and forth, his hands to his face, the blood trickling between his fingers.

"You three dopes, up against that wall," I said. "Lean your backs on it. Now walk away."

They did as I said until they were leaning on the wall and would have to move their feet and arms and lunge to stand up.

"You too, Red, and don't bleed on my rug." Red moved over, still holding his nose.

"Now," I said, "you, Muscles. You ready to continue yet?"

He was still on his knees, but he'd raised his head.

"What do you mean?" he said. His voice was strained with discomfort.

"You ready to teach me a lesson in race relations?" I said.

"You didn't have a gun," he said.

"Sure," I said. "If I didn't have a gun I could fight five of you. That seems fair."

"If you hadn't kicked me," he mumbled.

"I'd have punched you like I did Red and you'd have blood all over your pectoral muscles. You ready to stand up yet?"

"Yeah." He got painfully to his feet and looked at me with his head half lowered. "We won't forget this," he said.

"No, I certainly hope not," I said. "But I'm still game for a couple of rounds, if you like."

"You holding the gun?"

"Sure, just so I don't have to deal with all five of you at once. So I'll fight you one-handed. How's that sound?"

"Sure, till I start winning, then you use the gun, right?"

125

"You won't start winning, so the question is moot," I said.

"You think you can fight me one hand?"

"Sure," I said, and hit him square in the nose with my left fist. It rocked him back and the blood started. Just like Red. He shook his head and started toward me.

"You on the wall, you start to move and I'll kill you," I said, and rolled backwards and let his right fist sweep past my chin. I hooked my left hand over his right shoulder and caught him on the cheek under his right eye. I did it twice more, short hooks before he could get his right shoulder and arm up for cover. When he raised the right arm I slid around him with a little shuffle and got a sharp hook into his kidneys. He grunted and turned toward me, and I slapped the gun from my right to my left hand and hit him full swinging straight overhand right on the chin, and he sagged and rubber-legged backwards two steps and sat down, his legs spread and flaccid, his arms sagging in his lap. He sat for a minute, then went over on his side and was still.

One of the wall birds, a guy with a thick neck and very blond hair, said, "You said one hand."

"At a time," I said.

I put the gun back in my right hand. My knuckles were a little numb and would probably be puffy tomorrow. There was a pleasant touch of sweat on my forehead and the muscles in my shoulders and back felt energized and engorged. I felt good. Watch out, Red Rose, I'm on your trail.

"Get him on his feet," I said, "and get him out of here."

Red held on to his nose. The other three got the weight

lifter to his feet and helped him as he wobbled among them. All five looked like they were trying to find a way to leave with dignity.

One of them, the blond one, said, "We know where you are."

I said, "You knew where I was this time, and look what it got you." No one had anything to add to that, so they shuffled the weight lifter through the door and were gone.

I put the gun back under my arm, went to the sink in the washroom and ran cold water over my hands for a few minutes, and rinsed my face and toweled dry. Then I went back into my office and walked to the window and looked down at Berkeley Street where it intersects Boylston and did some deep breathing.

. . . It seemed like he could trust her. He could talk to her about things he'd never said before. About that time in school. About his mother. She never told. They weren't supposed to. There was some sort of oath . . . it never hurts to keep your mouth shut.

"My mother used to say that women would take me for all they could get."

She smiled slightly and nodded.

"I guess she meant money. That they'd go out with me for my money."

"Did you have a lot of money?"

"Me? No. My father had some, but I never had any, and, I mean, I was a kid; kids don't have money."

Today she was wearing a light gray suit with a high round collar and some pearls. Her stockings and shoes were white.

"So maybe there was something else they'd take," she said.

"Like what?"

She shrugged.

"I always felt bad when she said that. It was like nobody would go out with me for, you know, just what they could get. And it made me feel like I was stupid, like if any broad wanted to take me for everything she could get, she could, and I'd be too weak to stop her."

"Weak," she said. It wasn't exactly a question, and it wasn't exactly a comment.

"Dumb, whatever."

She nodded.

"Must have made girls seem pretty scary, when you were a boy."

"Well, not scary. I mean a boy doesn't have to be scared of a girl."

"Um hmm."

"I used to fantasize sometimes." He would feel the surge of passion, almost ejaculatory, as he flitted closer to revelation. "I used to think about tying them up." He could barely speak for the rush of excitement. He felt the sexual thrill of it dance through him.

"Um hmm."

They were both quiet. I could tie you up, he thought. If I had my stuff with me. I could make you stay there and tie you up.

"What do you suppose those girls were going to take?" she said again. He felt as if he might explode.

"Me," he heard his voice. "They'd take me."

"Away from?" she said.

"Her." His voice seemed loose from him, out there on its own in the room.

21

Susan and I were having dinner in Davio's on Newbury Street, in a booth in the back. Susan had developed a taste for red wine, so that lately she was putting away a glass at a single sitting. We had a bottle of Chianti between us and a salad each.

Susan guzzled nearly a gram of Chianti and put the glass down.

"Um," she said.

"We've got a list of seven possibles among your clients," I said.

"Possible Red Rose killer?"

"Possible guy who left the rose and ran."

"How did you come by the list?" she said.

"We staked out the office and followed anyone who fit the description."

"Who's we?"

"Quirk, Belson, and me. Hawk stayed with you."

"Because you were the man who'd seen him," she said.

"Yes."

"Did you compromise them?"

"No," I said. "They never knew they were followed." I handed her the seven names typed on a piece of white paper. She picked up the paper without looking at it.

"Of course I speculated on who it could be," she said. "To outrun you they had to fall within certain broad categories."

I nodded. There was some bread in a basket on the table and I broke off a piece and used it as a pusher when I ate some salad.

She looked at the list. Nodded her head.

"Yes," she said. "These were some I considered. You must have eliminated others because they didn't look like the man you chased—height, that sort of thing."

"Yes."

"It is unfortunate as hell," Susan said, "that our professional lives have had to intersect like this, so soon after we had reorganized our personal lives."

"I know," I said. "But we have to deal with it. We've dealt with worse."

"Yes," she said, and took another hit on the Chianti. "We have. And we can. It's just that the problem cuts across business and personal in a way that touches on the core of our relationship."

"I know," I said.

"We are able to love one another with the intensity that we do because we are able to be separate while we are at the same time one."

131

"E Pluribus Unum?" I said.

"I think that's something else," Susan said.

The salads went and pasta came. When the waiter had set down the food and left, Susan said, "This thing is compromising the separateness. I'm never alone. If you're not with me, Hawk is. And when I'm working, one of you is there, at the top of the stairs with a gun."

I nodded. I was having linguine with clam sauce. It was elegant.

"You know that this has nothing to do with being tired of you," Susan said. She had her fork in her hand and was leaning forward over her tortellini.

"Yes," I said. "I know that."

"Or Hawk," Susan said. "There is no one except you I enjoy being with more than Hawk."

"But you need time alone."

"Absolutely."

"But," I said, "we can't let him kill you."

Susan smiled.

"No. We can't," she said. "And I'm quite confident that we won't. If I'm to be guarded, who better?"

We ate pasta.

"If one of my patients is in fact the Red Rose killer, and left the rose in my hallway, I could probably make a stab at which of these names it is," Susan said.

"But you aren't going to," I said.

"I can't." She ate some more tortellini. "Yet."

"Remember that it's not only you. It might be some unknown black woman that he's going to do next."

Susan nodded. "That of course also weighs with me. This is very difficult." She drank some wine. "He has not

132

struck, if you'll pardon the melodramatic statement, since Washburn confessed."

"We both know the answer to that," I said.

"Yes. He could lie low for a while."

"But how long?" I said.

"He'd probably be able to hold off for a while, but . . . it's need. The poor bastard is driven by a need he cannot resist. He's acting out something awful."

"So he'll do it again."

"Yes," Susan said softly. "And God only knows what going under cover costs him, and what he'll be like when he emerges."

"You think he's one of yours," I said.

She looked at the wine in her glass. The light above the booth shone through it and made it ruby. Then she looked back up at me and nodded slowly.

"I think he's one of mine."

"Which one?" I said.

She shook her head.

"I haven't the right," she said. "Not yet. If I'm wrong and he's accused, it will destroy him."

"Godammit," I said.

Susan reached across the table and put her hands on my mouth. She let her hands slide down from my mouth along my shoulders and arms and rested them on my forearms.

"Please," she said. "Please."

I took in as much air as I could get through my nose and let it out slowly, the way I used to let cigarette smoke drift out after I inhaled. She was leaning forward so far that the tortellini was in danger.

"To be who I am. To be the woman you love, to be part of what we are, which is not like anyone else is, to be Susan, I have to be able to deal with this as I must. I must use my judgment and my skill and I mustn't let fear change any of that."

I looked at her small hands lying on my forearms. It seemed as if we were alone in a void, no waiters, no diners, no restaurant, no world. And it seemed as if we sat that way for twenty minutes.

"No," I said finally, "you mustn't. You're perfectly right."

I looked up at her big eyes, and they held me. She smiled slowly.

"And," I said, "you're about to put your tit in the tortel-lini."

. . . He'd heard the boyfriend on the radio, Spenser. He'd been saying that the schwartze didn't do it. Did they know about him? Did the sonovabitch make him when he'd left the rose? Everybody else thought the schwartze did it. How come Spenser didn't? Did she? Did she know he did it? Did she know he tied all the other broads up and gagged them and watched them struggle and try to scream through the gag? He looked at the fish in the tank swimming quietly, the morning sun shining through the tank. She'd come out in a minute and say come in and then he'd be in the tank. Maybe she'd like being tied up. Some women did. They liked being tied up and naked and begging for it. He could feel the rush again as he thought about it. But he couldn't come talk to her anymore if he did something. And she might tell the boyfriend. Big bastard. In the papers it said he'd been a fighter. Fuck him. Maybe she'd told the boyfriend. Maybe she suspected him from what he said in there. They knew. Shrinks knew stuff even when you didn't want them to. She watched him all the time. She watched when he moved his arm or jiggled his foot, or shifted in the chair. She watched everything. She concentrated on him . . . the fish cruised in slow circles in the sunny water . . . she cared about him. She wouldn't tell the boyfriend. She wouldn't. The boyfriend thought it on his own. The bas-

135

tard. She wouldn't tell. The office door opened. She was there in a dark blue dress with red flowers on it.

"Come in," she said.

When he stood, it startled the fish and they darted about in the tank.

"My father used to go to whores," he said. "And then he'd feel bad about it and the next day he'd bring her roses."

The shrink seemed interested. He thought she would be.

"And she used to say, 'You been with some floozie, George?' And he'd just sort of look at the floor and say, 'A rose for you, Rosie,' and he'd go away."

"He wouldn't fight with her," the shrink said.

"No, he never fought with her. He just got drunk and went to the whores."

She looked quietly at him. There was always that quiet about her, that peaceful welcoming stillness. No judgments.

"How did you feel about that?" she said.

He felt himself shrugging, felt himself being casual.

"Hell, he took me once," he said. He felt the feeling again in his stomach, the feeling of voidness. She raised her eyebrows slightly. "Black hooker," he said. "I was about fourteen." The void was expanding and behind it the sensation, the hotness and tingle that always came. He heard himself telling her. He felt his daring and that added to the tingle. "Christ, she smelled bad."

The shrink waited, inviting him with her calmness.

"Turned me off," he said, still feeling himself being casual.

They were both quiet, the shrink sitting perfectly still,

136

he sitting as casually as he could, one arm leaning on the back of his chair. He could feel his eyes begin to tear. Still casual, he looked at her, blurred now, waiting.

"I couldn't," he said, his voice shaky and hoarse. "I couldn't do anything. She was fat, and, and . . ." He felt his shoulders shake a little. ". . . hairy and . . . she was mean."

"To you?" the shrink said.

"Yes." So he was telling her. "Yes. She teased me and talked about how little it was and how weak it was and she tried to make me do it, tried, you know, to make me hard, and I couldn't and she got mad and said I was insulting her and I better do it or she'd cut it off and I was a bigot 'cause she was black."

"Terrifying," the shrink said.

"And my father was off somewhere fucking some other whore and I couldn't get away."

He struggled for breath. The sentences had been too long.

"And," the shrink said.

"And finally she threw me out of the room with no pants on and locked the door. And I had to wait there until my father came and took me home with his jacket wrapped around me. And some of the other whores saw me."

"Did you talk about this with your father?"

"He was mad at me for losing my pants. He said my mother would be mad at us."

137

22

Belson came by Susan's place at eleven in the morning and gave me a thick folder that had everything he and Quirk had learned about all seven suspects.

"Quirk says read it and think about it and then we should talk," Belson said. "You, me, Quirk, and Susan, if she will."

"Okay, I'll do it today," I said. "What are you going to do?"

"Go home, introduce myself to the wife and kids, and take a nap."

"Before you do that," I said, "see if you can compare this voice to the one I gave you before."

"Red call you again?"

"Among others. You'll see which one I mean. It's the one that says he might still be out there."

"I'll see if we can get an unofficial voiceprint even though I'm on vacation," Belson said. "I'll let you know."

Belson left and I began to read. Most of them were notable for not being interesting. There were no arrest records among them. Iselin, the Eastern studies prof, had had a jam while instructing in a private boys' school. A student had complained that Iselin solicited him, but nothing seemed to come of it. Two years later Iselin finished his Ph.D. at Harvard and stayed on to teach. Larson, the cop, had applied for sick leave, pleading burn-out, and been told to seek counseling. All were married except Felton and Iselin. Iselin had never been married, and Felton was divorced. They'd already eliminated Larson, the cop, because his work record showed he'd been on duty and accountable during the time at least three of the murders had happened. Gagné, the Frenchman, was out too. He'd been in France visiting his family when the second murder took place during Harvard spring break. Of the five remaining, Felton, the security guard, jumped out. There were two college teachers, a medical intern, the owner of a gourmet food store, and a security guard. We could probably eliminate a couple of others if we could talk with them or their co-workers. We could establish if Charles, the intern, had been on duty during any of the murders, for instance. But then they'd know they were being gumshoed. I liked Felton. I took his folder and read it again. There's only a little you can do in a short time without creating suspicion. He was forty-three years old, divorced, father deceased. Current address was Charlestown, but he had grown up in Swampscott. There was a Xerox of a page from his high school yearbook. His picture was there among others and his school activities were listed.

"Son of a bitch," I said.

Under his picture it said Track 3, 4. Didn't prove any-thing. That was twenty-five years ago. But still. I put down the file and got on the phone and talked with the AD at Swampscott High School.

"Kid named Gordon Felton," I said. "Ran on your track team there in . . . it would be 1961 and 1962. What did he run?"

The AD said, "Why do you want to know?"

"Name's Arthur Daley," I said. *"New England Sports Weekly.* We're doing a retrospective. High school sports twenty-five years ago."

"Hey, nice idea. Hang on, I can check on it in a minute. We got pictures and stuff back to the war."

He was gone maybe five minutes while I listened to the sound of silence on the wires. What a great idea. It could replace Muzak.

Then the AD came back on. "Mr. Daley. Yeah, Gordie Felton was a hurdler. Third in the state in the 440 high hurdles."

"Thanks," I said. "You don't know where he is now, do you?"

"Naw, I've only been here three years. I just got it out of the files."

"Okay," I said. "Thanks for your help."

We hung up. It still didn't prove anything. Because he could do it then didn't mean he could do it now. Still, a lot of men can't outrun me, and the guy that left the Red Rose could.

I read all the folders again except Larson and Gagné, and read them again and then put them down and stood and walked around Susan's place, looking out the windows, checking the refrigerator, looking out the windows on the other side. The refrigerator had a head of cauliflower, some broccoli, two Diet Cokes, and a package of Chinese noodles. *Bon appétit.*

Hawk showed up at one with tuna fish subs, everything but onions, and a large bag of Cape Cod potato chips.

"I wish we'd catch the bastard," Hawk said. "I'm getting rock-jolly sitting around here every day."

He was wearing a brown Harris tweed sport coat and a blue oxford-weave button-down shirt with no tie and three buttons open. His jeans were starched and ironed and he had on mahogany cowboy boots.

"What are you today," I said, "a Harvard cowboy?"

"Eclectic," Hawk said, and began unrolling one of the subs. We ate at Susan's island, leaning over the unwrapped paper to keep from slopping on the counter.

"One of the guys on the list used to be a hurdler in high school," I said. "Was third in the state in his senior year."

"Must have been a while back or he'd a been a brother," Hawk said.

"Nineteen sixty-two," I said.

Hawk nodded. "Don't mean a hell of a lot," he said.

"He's a security guard," I said.

"Maybe wish he were a cop?" Hawk said.

"Might even claim to be," I said.

"How she doing?" Hawk said. When he talked "she" he always meant Susan.

"She thinks she has an idea who our man might be," I said, "but she can't be sure."

"So she sit and listen to him and nod and let him talk

and she don't know for sure he won't stick a handgun in her and pull the trigger," Hawk said.

"Which is why she has one of us baby-sitting twenty-four hours a day," I said. "She's getting sort of rock-jolly too."

Hawk nodded. "Time to review the evidence again?"

"Yeah. The hurdler has an ex-wife," I said. "Maybe I'll go talk with her."

"Take my picture along," Hawk said. "Tell her she can meet me if she cooperate."

"And if she doesn't," I said, "she meets you twice."

23

Mimi Felton lived in a condo in a vast assemblage of town houses clustered around a man-made pond in Concord. That morning on the phone she told me that she worked the makeup counter at Bloomingdale's and didn't go to work until four. I got there at 2:10 and she answered my knock wearing a white ribbed-cotton halter and black jeans, which she must have zipped lying down. She was barefoot. She had a lot of blond hair combed so as to show me she had a lot of blond hair. She had rings on eight fingers, and her earrings dangled like Christmas ornaments from her ears.

"Hi," she said. "Mr. Spenser, come in."

She had a lot of good makeup expertly applied and false eyelashes. Her nails, finger and toe, were painted some tone of dark purple. Her bare midriff was firm and tan and flat.

"So you're a detective?"

"Yes," I said. "I need you to tell me what you can about Gordon Felton."

"Could I see your badge, or license, or whatever they give you," she said. She had a little-girl voice that stopped just this side of lisping. I showed her my license.

"Why do you want to know about Gordie?" she said.

"Routine," I said. "Since he works for a security firm, the bonding company occasionally runs a check on the employees they're bonding."

"That's like insurance," she said in her little voice. It was the kind of voice that went with a curtsy.

"Yeah."

"Well, you look like you could bond anyone you wanted, Mr. Spenser."

"Sure," I said. "What happened to cause your divorce, Mrs. Felton?"

"Here, sit down," she said, and we walked into her small living room. There were avant-garde art prints on the walls, and all the colors were lavender and gray. The little picture window gave us a glimpse of the artificial pond. She sat on a chair made of lavender canvas on a triangular black iron frame. There were two others grouped around a massive Mediterranean coffee table that must have come from the house in Swampscott.

"I'll stand, thanks. What about the divorce?"

"Gordie," she said. "Gordie, Gordie, Gordie . . ."

"That was it?" I said.

"What?"

144

"How come you got divorced?" I said.

She shook her head. "He was such a little boy," she said. "Always acting so macho and being such a sissy."

"Like what?" I said.

"Well, he wouldn't go anywhere alone, without me," she said.

"How about the macho stuff?" I said.

"He used to carry a gun. He wanted to be a policeman, but I don't think he ever really applied for a police job. He always talked about it. He was like a police groupie, you know. Had the scanner radio, and hung around the cops in Swampscott when we were married. And anytime he'd hear some crime, something on the scanner, he'd get in the car and go to the scene, he was weird."

"Family?" I said.

"We never had children," Mimi said.

"How about his family?" I said.

"How come you're not writing all this down?" she said.

I tapped my temple. "Once it's in the computer," I said, "it's there for eternity."

She nodded. "His father's dead," she said. "His mother's still alive. Lives in Swampscott." Mimi shook her head.

"Why the head shake?" I said.

"God, he hates her," she said.

"His mother?"

"Yes," Mimi shook her head again, and smiled without any pleasure.

"Blackie's a piece of work," she said.

"Blackie?"

"Gordie's mother."

145

"Why is she called Blackie?" I said.

"Her maiden name: Rose Mary Black," Mimi said. "Everybody always called her Blackie."

"Jesus Christ," I said.

24

"It's Felton," I said.

Susan and Hawk and I sat at Susan's counter on Saturday morning, drinking coffee and eating whole-wheat bagels that Hawk had picked up at Fromaggio on his way over.

On the counter was an 8 1/2 × 11 brown manila envelope that Hawk had got from Belson before he made the bagel run. It contained a voiceprint matchup of the two phone messages and a tape of both messages side by side.

Susan took a jar of cherry preserves from the refrigerator under the counter and put it out with the cream cheese. She spread a vaporously thin layer of cream cheese on a small piece of bagel she'd broken off. She dabbed a minuscule of preserve on it and took a small bite.

"It is, Susan," Hawk said.

"Yes," Susan said when she swallowed her morsel of bagel. "It probably is."

I stirred a spoonful of sugar into my second cup of coffee.

"It explains the symbolism," I said. "The red rose, the black women. Rose Mary Black, aka Blackie."

Susan carefully sliced a bagel in two and put both halves in her imported German toaster, which was wide enough to contain two bagel slices. She slid the toast lever down.

"I knew her first name was Rose," Susan said. "But he never mentioned his mother's last name."

"Isn't that unusual?" I said.

"Not really, many patients talk of 'my wife,' 'my mother,' 'my father'—particularly parents, whom the patient has never really thought of by their name."

The toaster popped and Susan took the bagels out and put them on Hawk's plate.

"And he was having trouble with her, wasn't he?" I said.

Susan watched Hawk put cream cheese on his bagel. Like everything else Hawk did, it was done without wasted motion, without mistake, and there was exactly the right amount. When Hawk ate pizza he never got any on his tie.

"If he was in the grip of some sort of unresolved rage at his mother," Susan said, "and his mother's name was Rose Mary Black, and there were other factors that I know, a man might in fact express that rage in a deflected manner on people who could appropriately symbolize Rose Mary Black."

"Like black women," Hawk said, "and leave a rose."

"Yes," Susan said, "and if the object of his rage was

148

infinitely powerful, the rage would be overlaid with fear. And if the rage and fear were sexually inspired and sexually expressed, it might have to be in a kind of surrogation."

"You mean, he might have to tie them up and rape them with a gun," I said.

"Yes," Susan said. She was drinking her coffee, holding the mug in both hands, watching me over the rim.

"Does Felton fit that kind of a profile?" I said.

Susan continued to look at me over the rim of her cup. She sipped a little decaffeinated coffee. She had a faux art clock that ran on a battery, on the coffee table in the living room, and its ticking was loud and metronomic. Hawk poured some more coffee into his cup and then added some to mine.

I looked at Susan. She looked at me and then closed her eyes.

"Yes," she said. "He fits it better than you can know."

I said, "We've got a tape that Belson did a voiceprint on. One's the guy that called and said he was Red Rose and challenged me. The other came after the Jimmy Winston fiasco. Voiceprint says they're the same."

Susan nodded. "I'll listen," she said.

I went to her stereo and put the tape in. Susan listened with her chin in her hand. I played the two conversations three times.

Susan still sat with her chin in her hand, staring at the tape machine. Hawk and I waited. Susan blew her breath out in a short burst.

"It sounds like him," she said. "No certainty, it could be someone else, but it could be him."

I took the tape out of the stereo. Hawk sat in repose, stool tipped back, balanced lightly with his elbows against the edge of the counter. I was pretty sure he didn't really need the counter.

Susan took her chin from her hand. "I too know it's him," she said. "But there's nothing I can say in terms of courtroom-type evidence. Because these crimes fit a man with his pathologies, it doesn't mean he committed them. I've had many men with similar pathologies that are able to master them."

"What makes the difference?" Hawk said.

"I don't know," Susan said. "Character, influences of other people in their lives, degree of Oedipal manipulation on the mother's part, intelligence of the patient, will to succeed in the therapy, blind chance." Susan smiled. "All of the above."

"How 'bout divine intervention," Hawk said.

"Wouldn't it be pretty," Susan said.

Hawk smiled at her with warmth that no one ever got.

"He's the one," I said.

"Yes," Hawk said.

"Yes," Susan said.

"And we can't prove it," I said.

"The voiceprint?" Susan said.

"Just proves that the same guy called me twice. Doesn't prove he's Red Rose. Doesn't prove the guy they've got for it isn't Red Rose. Even if you could identify the voice without equivocation, it wouldn't prove he was Red Rose."

"Equivocation," Hawk said.

"Keep hanging around with me," I said to Hawk. "Listen and learn."

"My appointment book will show that Felton was there the day that you chased him," Susan said.

"So were, what, seven other people?" I said.

She nodded.

"What about the murders?" Hawk said.

"The murders?" Susan said.

"Compare the dates of his therapy with the dates of the murders," I said.

"Why?"

"See what happen," Hawk said. "We know the fish in there, we casting around trying to find where."

"I'll get my book," Susan said. She left us and went down to the office.

Hawk said, "We can't prove this guy did it, but we know he did. Sooner or later we got to do something."

"I know," I said.

Susan came back with her appointment book.

"What are the murder dates?" she said.

I knew them by heart and told her.

She wrote them down in her attractive and completely unreadable hand. It was graceful and composed of well-integrated linear sweeps, which had great surface charm and no intelligibility. Susan's handwriting was so bad that often she couldn't read it herself when she went back to it later.

She leafed through her appointment book while Hawk and I cleared the counter and rinsed the cups and put them in the dishwasher. I capped the cherry preserves and put the top back on the cream cheese container and

151

put them in the refrigerator. Hawk was washing his hands and face at the sink and drying them on a paper towel.

"Sonovabitch," Susan said.

Hawk and I turned and looked at her.

"Felton normally comes twice a week," Susan said. "The days vary, but the twice a week doesn't. All the murders except the first were on the day after an appointment."

"When did he start therapy?" I said.

"Two weeks after the first one," Susan said.

The room was quiet. The wet hum of the dishwasher was all there was to listen to.

"Something in the sessions must have set him off," Susan said.

I could feel the faint tremor in the floor as the dishwasher went about its business.

"Doesn't have to mean that," Hawk said.

"I know," Susan said. She was entirely Dr. Silverman now, thinking about human behavior. "But the coincidence is startling."

"What would have done it?" I said.

Susan shook her head. She walked to the window and stared down at Saturday morning on Linnaean Street. We were quiet. Hawk settled back onto his stool, I stood with my back to the sink, leaning against it. Susan turned finally and looked at us.

"Me, I think."

"How so?" I said.

"I probably wasn't the right referral for him. An attractive older woman in a position of authority, it was easy for the transference of feelings from his mother onto me."

"That one of the things supposed to happen?" Hawk said.

"Yes, and I'm supposed to then lead him to master those feelings, because I'm not his mother and our interaction will not nurture his condition."

"But here?" I said.

"Here his passion for his mother was transferred to me and her unattainability existed as well in me, and, my God, it's a seminar in shrink school, but, too simply, his need for oblique and symbolic sex-slash-punishment was simply intensified by the transference plus the unfortunate accident of your relationship with both the case and me."

"Laius to your Jocasta?" I said.

Susan nodded.

Hawk said, "I just a poor simple minority pistolero. You intellectuals talking 'bout Oedipus?"

"I told you you'd learn stuff," I said.

"Grateful for the chance, bawse," Hawk said.

Susan was fully engaged with her topic and paid no attention to us.

"I should have given him a referral," she said. "I could feel the erotic tension in our first interview."

"But you figured you could handle it," I said.

"And help him master it," Susan said.

"And in time you probably could have," I said.

"And four women dead," she said. "We have no more time."

153

. . . Her boyfriend had been to see Mimi. He'd lied about some kind of bonding check, but it was him. Big, tough-looking guy, broken nose, just like the boyfriend. She'd been telling on him. She must know. He felt as if he would come off like an explosion. She knows. He felt like he did when he did the colored girls. Pull the trigger and feel the explosion . . . the bitch. She told. She fucking told. There was no one to trust. His mother, his wife—ex-wife— Her. They all fucked you up one way or another. . . . He thought about bound black women. The fantasy always helped when he was upset. He thought about putting his stuff in the gym bag, the tape, the rope, the gun. He thought about the shrink with her black hair and dark eyes. Maybe I should do them all, he thought, maybe I should do them all together, all in the same room. He thought of his wife—ex-wife—helpless on the floor. He thought of Her. He was standing above them. He went to the hidden place he'd made, removed the section of base-board and took out the gun. A .38 caliber Smith & Wesson, nickel-plated, walnut grips, 4-inch barrel, unregistered. His registered gun was in the bedroom closet in his hol-ster, hanging beside his uniform. He'd taken this one from his mother's house after his father's funeral. She never knew he took it. He took his father's gun and put it in the gym bag. From his hiding place he took the roll of

clothesline and the duct tape and put them in the bag. He didn't know what he was going to do yet, but he was getting ready. He felt strong and full to have his trouble bag ready. Maybe the boyfriend. Maybe if he weren't around he could take his time with Her. The sense of fullness went away. His stomach felt hollow. He took the gun from the bag and hefted it. He turned toward the mirror on the far wall and went into a crouch, looking at himself over the gun sight. The handle of the gun was smooth and solid. The gun sight didn't waver. His stomach felt better. But it didn't feel good. He thought about the women some more and the full feeling came back. He turned sideways and watched himself in the mirror as he aimed one-handed, in profile, and then full face again. It had been a long time since the last one. The hell with them. He needed it. He looked at himself aiming into the mirror and thought about Dr. Silverman.

25

Susan and I had one of the larger fights we'd had. It started when she said, "I cannot of course continue as his therapist." And I said, "Absolutely not."

"He has an appointment Monday, and I'll have to tell him we cannot continue under the current circumstances," she said.

"Sure," I said. "When's his appointment?"

Susan had her book open on the counter.

"Eleven," she said. "I'll be in the office," I said, "and Hawk will be in the waiting room."

She said, "No."

"Yes."

"No. I cannot have a patient come in for what he thinks will be therapy to be confronted with two armed men."

"He's killed four women," I said. "I cannot let you tell him you know he did it without being around to protect you."

"I'm afraid you'll have to," Susan said. "You and Hawk both may stay up here as you have. I won't have you in the office. He has a right to that sanctuary."

"And I have a right to keep you alive," I said.

Susan slammed her hand down flat on top of the counter.

"Don't you, God damn it, play God with me," she said.

We were silent, looking at each other. Hawk sat comfortably, watching without expression. As far as you could tell from his reaction, we could have been discussing my plans for a haircut.

"I won't let you be alone with him," I said. "We worked too hard. It cost too much, to be who we are, to risk it for professional ethics, or human compassion, or your sense of self or all of them and world peace thrown in."

"You won't *let* me?" she said.

"I won't let you."

"Who the hell are you to talk about letting me?" she said.

"Your Sweet Patootie," I said.

Hawk was shifting his gaze uninterestedly back and forth between us, like a man watching a tennis match that didn't matter.

Susan said to him, "Have you got anything to say?"

"I won't let you be alone with him either," Hawk said.

Susan patted the fingertips of both hands along the edge of the counter. She looked down as she did so and studied her hands while they moved back and forth along the countertop.

"His rights stop this side of us," I said.

"And mine?" Susan said.

157

I shook my head. "I won't get metaphysical about this. I'm bigger, I can insist, and I do."

She studied her tapping fingers some more. I waited. I could see her breathing begin to slow. Hawk took a plum from the bowl. Hawk finished the plum and got up and dropped the pit into the wastebasket and sat down. Susan's breathing was quiet now. She looked up.

"You are my Sweet Patootie," she said. "You can be with me when I talk with Felton."

"Thank you," I said.

"You're welcome."

Hawk smiled benignly, like a proud grandparent.

"Knew you two could work it out," he said.

"Oh, fuck you," Susan said.

"Good point," Hawk said.

26

At nine minutes to eleven on Monday a blond young woman with what amounted to a crew cut came out of Susan's office and took her yellow slicker off the rack and went out of the waiting room without looking at me. As soon as the door closed behind her I got up and went into Susan's office. Hawk lingered at the top of the stairs. As soon as Felton showed up in the waiting room, Susan would ask him to come into the office, and as soon as he came in Hawk would come downstairs and sit in the waiting room.

"He always comes at one minute to eleven," Susan had said. "There's never anyone waiting. If he sees Hawk in the waiting room, it will frighten him."

"Does it matter?" I had said. "Hawk won't let him leave."

"You have forced your protection on me," Susan had said. "That's enough."

Which was why I was standing on the wall behind the door as Felton entered and Hawk waited until he was in to come sit in the waiting room. Susan was wearing a dark blue suit with a boxy jacket and a white sweater. She stood when the waiting-room door opened and walked without hesitation to the office door and said, "Come in." Then she walked back into the office and stood by the doorway. When Felton entered, Susan closed the double layered door behind him. Then she went around her desk and sat down. Felton stood where he'd entered, looking at me. I looked back. It was the first time we'd met in daylight.

Susan said, "Sit down, please, Mr. Felton. I will explain in a moment why Mr. Spenser is here."

Felton continued looking at me, and I at him. He was probably six feet tall, maybe a little less, and slim, with a springiness in his bearing that suggested he was in decent shape. His brown hair was receding on each side of a widow's peak and there was a balding crown at the back. He had an untrimmed mustache that would have been bushy if he had the whiskers for it, but his beard was too light and it was merely untidy.

"Sit down, please, Mr. Felton," Susan said. Her voice was clear and firm.

Felton turned and sat in the chair beside her desk. He could see me from there and Susan too. I folded my arms and leaned against the wall. I kept my face blank. The thing about monsters is, you want to kill them until you meet them, and when you meet them they don't seem monstrous, and killing them begins to seem unkind.

"What's the situation here?" Felton said to Susan.

"I'm sorry to bring Mr. Spenser in here, but we felt it

necessary. I am convinced that you are the serial killer who uses a red rose for a trademark," Susan said. "Thus it seemed in my own best interests to have Mr. Spenser here, and another gentleman in the waiting room, while we discussed this."

Felton looked at me and back at Susan. He opened his mouth and closed it. I could see his face struggle to look contemptuous and contained.

"I hope you will confess," Susan said, "to me, and to the police. If you do, I will stand by you, but I cannot continue, under present conditions, as your therapist."

"You're kicking me out because you think I'm the killer?" Felton said.

I noticed he didn't say red rose, simply "the killer."

"Surely if we've gotten anyplace in here," Susan said, "we have come to understand that the way things are said matters. I am not kicking you out, I am withdrawing from my role as therapist. How effective do you suppose I could be if I continued, convinced you were a serial murderer and, frankly, apprehensive for my own safety?"

Felton's body was very tight. He sat up very straight and clasped his hands before him, his elbows resting on the arms of his chair. The posture made his shoulders hunch up somewhat. He seemed to feel hunched because he stretched his neck to its full length when he spoke.

"Well, you can't prove anything like that," he said.

"No, I can't," Susan said. "Nor is it my work to do so, nor will I share the confidences of our therapy with the police or anyone else. But I will tell the police that I am convinced of your guilt, as I'm convinced that you left the rose for me, as I'm convinced you killed the fish in my waiting room."

"You can't stop seeing me," he said.

"I'm sorry," Susan said.

"I didn't do anything. You can't. You got a responsibility. You took some kind of oath or something."

Susan shook her head slightly. "I am not an M.D. I am a Ph.D. I could not continue, however, even had I taken the Hippocratic oath."

"I have to talk to someone," Felton said. "I got no one to talk to. There has to be somebody."

"If you will tell the truth, we can talk, but it has to be the truth and it has to be shared with the police and the courts. If you tell the truth, I will argue as persuasively as I know how that you need treatment, not electrocution. But I cannot, obviously, guarantee what the courts would decide."

Felton was still rigid in his chair. But his face was pale and his eyes were full of tears.

"Who will I talk to?" he said.

"I can do no further good for you," Susan said.

"I can't. You have to. I didn't do it, don't you believe me? I didn't."

Susan was quiet. Felton's rigidity began to loosen. He slumped in his chair and then bent forward as if there were no strength in his body to hold him upright.

"You can't," he said. His voice was thick and the tears that had come to his eyes were now running. "I can't stand it," he said. "I can't. Please don't do this. Don't leave me. There isn't anyone else. Don't. Don't."

Susan was still and her voice was steady and kind.

"If you don't confess, if you go on as you have, it will be worse for you, they will catch you soon." She nodded at me without looking at me. "He knows you are the killer. Pretty soon he will catch you."

Felton was rocking in his chair back and forward, bent double, sobbing. "I can't do it, I can't. You can't leave me."

"It is an awful choice for you," Susan said. "But it is a choice, and it is more than those four women had. You can confess and take your chances with my support, or you can leave now, and he," she nodded at me again, "and others will pursue you until you're caught."

Felton continued to rock and shake his head. "I didn't," he said. "I didn't." He slid forward out of the chair and pitched onto the floor and lay on his side with his knees up and his arms clutching himself.

"Jesus, oh, Jesus," he said. "I can't."

Susan got up from her chair and walked around her desk and crouched beside him and put her hand gently on his back.

"You can," she said. "Simply because you have no other choice."

He remained there and she remained beside him, her hand motionless on his back between his shoulder blades as he cried. It couldn't have gone on as long as it seemed, but after a while Felton got quiet. He sat up on the floor and then got slowly up, as if every bone ached, and stood holding on to the back of the chair with both hands.

"Okay," he said. "Okay. You fucking bitch, I can do it without you."

Below desk level, Susan turned the palm of her left hand toward me.

"When you are ready with the truth," Susan said, "I am here."

"I won't be back," Felton said. "You'll never humiliate me again. I'll get out of here and you and him can fuck on the couch over there like two dogs for all I care."

He turned and walked out the door into the waiting room. Hawk was leaning against the wall by the exit door. His eyes stayed on Felton without expression as Felton went to the door, opened it, went into the front hall and out the front door. Hawk went after him.

I closed the door.

Susan looked at me for a moment and began to cry, first a sniffle, then steadily, and then, head down on the desk, shoulders shaking. I started toward her and stopped, and knew something I didn't know how I knew, and waited quietly while she cried, and didn't touch her.

27

Susan took about ten minutes to get back together.

"Sorry about the tears," she said.

"Don't blame you," I said. "What you had to do was brutal."

"We're convinced he murdered four women," Susan said. "I doubt that he could stop himself, and I fear he won't be able to stop himself again. But that is little consolation to the four women, and the people that survived them."

"Hawk's behind him," I said.

"What if Felton loses him?"

"He won't. Hawk doesn't have to be circumspect. He doesn't have to keep from being spotted. He can walk along in Felton's shirt. He won't lose him."

"We can't let him kill someone else," Susan said.

"I know," I said. I took the phone off her desk and called

Quirk at home. His wife answered and in a moment Quirk came on.

"Felton's it, the security guard from Charlestown," I said.

"You sure?"

"I'm sure. I can't prove it, but I know it."

"Where is he now?" Quirk said.

"Just left Susan's office with Hawk behind him. Felton knows we know. Susan dropped him from therapy, he's in a lavender funk."

"I'll get Belson," Quirk said. "We'll see if we can pick him up at his home. You at Susan's?"

"Yeah."

"Stay there, I'll check with you in a while."

"I'll be here," I said.

We hung up.

"Quirk and Belson are going to join Hawk behind Felton," I said. "Then there will be three people on his tail and they can relieve each other."

"Until when?"

"Until we figure out a way to prove what he did," I said. "Then Quirk can arrest him and he's off the street."

"What if we can't prove it?"

"Eventually he has to be out of circulation," I said.

"You mean you will kill him, or Hawk will," Susan said.

"Quirk might," I said. "He can't be left loose."

"I know he is the killer."

"Yeah," I said.

"We must think of a way to catch him."

"Well," I said. "I'm not letting you out of my sight until we do, so let's begin. What about your other patients?"

"I cancelled my appointments for the rest of the day," Susan said.

"You want some lunch," I said.

"Yes," Susan said, "and probably two stiff drinks."

We went upstairs and I stirred up two vodka martinis with very little vermouth. Susan plunked three cocktail olives into a glass and I poured the martini over them. Susan picked up the glass, looked at it for a moment, and drank maybe a third of it in one swallow.

Susan's refrigerator was under the counter, and what it lacked in height it lacked also in width. I sat on my haunches to look for lunch possibilities. They were limited.

"There are a couple of boneless chicken breasts in the freezer," Susan said.

I found them on top of the ice trays. The ice trays were full. Normally Susan kept them in there empty. I put some extra virgin olive oil in a fry pan, took the foil off the chicken breasts, put the two small rocklike portions in the fry pan, poured some of the vermouth over them, covered the pan, and put it on the gas stove to simmer.

Susan was down two thirds in her martini.

I found a bottle of Laphroig single malt Scotch in her cupboard, beside a box of sugar cubes and in back of some all-natural peanut butter. I took it down, broke some ice cubes out of one of the plastic trays, and made a large Scotch-on-the-rocks.

"You were right, you know," Susan said.

"Probably," I said. "About what?"

Susan drank the rest of her martini and motioned with her glass. I poured her a second one and didn't even point out to her that I'd mixed without measuring and come out two glasses to the rim.

"About not letting me deal with Felton alone."

"It wasn't even right or wrong," I said. "I couldn't leave you alone."

"Just like you can't now," she said.

"Yes."

"Even though Hawk is following Felton, and Quirk and Belson will join him."

"Yes."

"Even though you told me Felton couldn't get away from Hawk."

"Yes."

"Why is that?" she said. She pulled the olive jar toward her and put two olives into her martini, which made it too full. She sipped some and put in another olive.

"I lost you for a couple of years back there," I said. "I found out that I could live without you. And I found out also that I didn't want to."

"Because?"

"Because I love you," I said. "Because you are in my life like the music at the edge of silence."

"The music what?"

"I never quite got it either," I said. "I read it somewhere."

I drank some of the Scotch. Susan drank some of the martini. The chicken breasts simmered, defrosting as they went. I mused through the refrigerator again, looking for inspiration. There was broccoli, and one carrot. Under the sink I found an onion, the last survivor in its mesh bag. I got the vegetables lined up and began to search for a knife.

"Let me try it another way," I said. "It is not only that I love you. It is that you complete my every shortfall."

Susan smiled and ate an olive.

"But do you respect me?" she said.

"I respect you like hell," I said. It was one of our thousand catch phrases, remembered from an old Nichols and May routine we'd each seen years before we knew each other. I found a paring knife and began to peel the onion.

"And," I said, "I complete yours. Our strengths and weaknesses interlock so perfectly that together we are more than the sum of our parts."

Susan smiled and ate another olive. Her martini was almost gone. Susan said, "Make some more martini."

I looked at her and raised my eyebrows and mixed up another batch.

"Thank you," Susan said when I filled her glass.

I drank some more of my Laphroig. If it was going to be like that, I didn't want to fall behind.

"It is one of the special ironies of love," Susan said. Her voice had a crystalline sound to it, as if it were coming through a clear filter. "All the received truths of popular culture presume that successful love is rooted in shared interests. Dating services computerize preference, hobbies, vacations, and such so that they can match like with like."

I had the onion peeled and was looking for a cutting board. I found it behind the toaster, a small fiberglass thing that looked as if it had never been cut on.

"And," Susan said, "in fact, of course, love frequently flourishes most successfully when ying meets yang."

"Ying meets yang?"

"Never mind," Susan said. "And just keep your ying to yourself."

I chopped the onion fine, and scraped the carrot and chopped it. I cut the broccoli into its component florets.

"It's why I was able to let you stay," Susan said.

She was sitting now with her chin in the palm of her hand. She took another olive from her martini and bit half of it off and chewed it while she looked at the other half.

"Stay with you and Felton?"

"Yes. Because it wasn't so much my need as yours."

"My weakness, so to speak."

"Un huh."

She ate the rest of the olive and drank the rest of the martini. I poured a little more Laphroig over ice. Susan poured more martini.

"And it didn't bother you," I said, "the implication that you couldn't handle it alone?"

"No," Susan said, looking hard at her martini. "Because the implication was true. I couldn't. Not if he attempted to tie me up and shoot me."

"You had a gun," I said.

"If I got to it in time."

I smiled suddenly. "For crissake," I said, "you wanted me there."

"Partly."

"You wanted me to insist. You wanted me to win the argument."

"Wanted is too simple," Susan said. She had shifted her

170

gaze from her martini to the ongoing afternoon outside her kitchen window. "I wanted and didn't want. I needed both my autonomy and your protection. By acting the way I did, I managed to have both."

I took the top off the fry pan and probed the chicken breasts with the tip of the paring knife. They appeared thawed. I swiped the carrots and onions off the cutting board and into the fry pan with the back of the knife. I added a clove of garlic and some dried tarragon and put the cover back on.

Susan drank the rest of her martini. Her pupils were very wide. She put the glass down and got off the stool and walked to me and leaned against me, with her arms around my waist. I put my arms around her and we stood like that for a time. Then Susan raised her face and I kissed her. She opened her mouth and tightened her arms and kissed me back for a long time. Then her body went nearly limp and she broke the kiss and hung her head back and looked up at me. Her pupils were now so big that her eyes seemed without iris.

"Bed," she said.

With my arms still around her I detached my left arm and shut off the flame under the chicken. Then I slid my left arm down her backside and scooped her into my arms. She pushed her head against my shoulder and locked her arms around my neck. I carried her through the living room and down the hall to her bedroom.

It's not as easy as it looked in *Gone With the Wind*.

Susan's bed was made of dark wicker and covered with a brown paisley spread, which she made up with the spread turned back, exposing a cobalt sheet. There were maybe eight oversized pillows covered in the same paisley. I eased her down onto the bed and she lay back flat with her arms out and her legs flaccid against the bed. She looked up at me with her eyes wide open. I took my gun from its holster and put it on the matching wicker table by the bed. I took off my clothes. Susan lay without movement, watching me. Only her eyes moved. Her body was without tension and seemed to be blending into the bed. Then I was undressed and she was fully clothed.

"Undress me," she said. Her voice was soft but it still had that odd clarity.

I nodded, feeling the little feeling I always did when I was undressed and my companion was not. I took Susan's shoes off. They were blue, with short heels. I put them carefully on the floor under the bed where neither of us would step on them. I got off her jacket. Susan made no move to help or hinder but lay loose and still, watching me with her huge unfocused eyes. The sweater had to come off over her head, and unless she helped it would present a problem. I started to raise her from the bed with my left hand under her shoulders.

"Leave the sweater," she said.

"Sure," I said. My voice sounded a little hoarse.

"Do the skirt," she said.

"Sure," I said. My voice was hoarser.

I've always been clever with my hands, and in a bit I had everything off but her sweater. Through it she lay as limp and passive as a teddy bear, her eyes wide open. I lay on my left side on the bed next to her and propped my head with my elbow.

"Now what?" I said.

She turned her head loosely on the pillow. Her un-focused eyes were looking through mine at something far away.

"Everything," she said.

28

It was a long, exploratory, surprising, flung-open afternoon, and when we were through Susan fell asleep on the bed, in her sweater. I got up, took my gun, and went into the kitchen and examined the chicken breasts. They had not suffered from marinating and might even have benefited. I let them sit and went to Susan's bathroom, put my gun on the toilet tank, moved three pairs of pantyhose, and took a shower. I shampooed with French Walnut Oil, which I found on the tub, and when I was through I put on the green terry cloth robe I keep there and took a bottle of club soda out from under the bathroom sink, where Susan kept it, picked up the gun, and went back to the kitchen. I made a light Scotch and soda and stood in her front window and looked out. The gun was on the coffee table behind me. Trees along Linnaean Street were beginning to bud. They were mostly maples, a few oak, and at least one horse chestnut. Across the street in front of the brick apartment building a Hispanic woman wearing a down vest over a print dress was rocking a baby in its carriage. She rolled the carriage back toward her and pushed it away as she leaned against the building. There was no sound in the apartment. I felt the sense of peace and disconnection that I felt after Susan and I made love. A Federal Express truck pulled up next door and a young woman in the FedEx uniform got out and headed up to the front door with one of those urgent-looking envelopes. Directly opposite me on the ledge outside the second story of the apartment building, four pigeons sat and craned their necks about and teetered like they do. I looked back down in the street. No one came along with a gun and a coil of rope.

"Goddamn," I said aloud in the quiet room.

If he'd make a move at us, I could kill him and it would be over. I didn't think Hawk would lose him and I didn't think Quirk would either. But it happens. It's very hard to stick with someone who knows you're there and who wants to lose you and doesn't care if you know he wants to lose you. If the guy you're tailing is resourceful, it is in fact impossible. I knew that and Quirk knew and Belson knew it. Hawk knew it, though Hawk never really believed that he could be thwarted.

It was why I wouldn't leave her.

I went back to the kitchen and made another light Scotch and soda, and walked back to the window and looked down some more.

What if he killed me?

I shook my head sharply. Thinking about that was too

painful. It wasn't too productive either. To be who I was and do what I did had to assume I'd win.

"Just because he could jump a fence better," I said. There was no other sound in the apartment.

It was like a lot of things: you felt fear not when it was most likely but when it was most awful. If he got past me to Susan . . . I shook my head again. He had to shake Hawk, and he had to be able to get past me. And he had to get Susan before she got the gun. Could she shoot? Yes. She could. If she had to. And if she had to, she'd be calm and steady and the gun wouldn't waver.

I looked down in the street again.

"Come on," I said. "Come on and do it."

I heard my own voice in the room and felt foolish, but my teeth were still clenched hard and the trapezius muscles were bunched up near my neck.

From the bed I heard Susan's voice.

"Hello," she said. It was a very small sound.

I walked down the hallway and into the bedroom. She lay on her back on top of the covers, wearing only her sweater.

I said, "It is wanton and shameless to make love while wearing a sweater."

She said, "Tell me there is a Diet Coke somewhere in this house."

"I saw one under the sink in the bathroom," I said. "I assume you want it warm."

"Yes, and at once," she said.

I went and got the Diet Coke and poured it into a large glass and got a lemon from the refrigerator and cut her a wedge and put it in the Coke. Actually I got a third of a lemon that had dried out slightly, which Susan had left in one of the egg-keeper pockets inside the door. I brought it to the bedroom and put it on the night table beside her bed. She was still flat on her back. I collected some of the pillows I had cast aside earlier and plumped them around her and put my hand behind her back between her shoulder blades and sat her up and slid the pillows behind her.

"Jesus Christ," she said.

I pushed the Diet Coke an inch closer to her. Her eyes slowly focused on it. She took it from the night table and drank and put it back. She was the only human I've ever seen who liked Diet Coke warm. She breathed deeply and let it out.

"What did you say about a sweater?" she said.

"I said it is wanton and shameless to make love while wearing a sweater."

"Yes," Susan said thoughtfully. "It is, isn't it."

She smiled at me. She said, "It's probably fairly shameless to lay around and drink Diet Coke wearing only a sweater."

"Yes," I said, "but a five-martini hangover thirst tends to humble even the best of us."

"Five?"

"Five."

"Good heavens," Susan said. She pulled her bare legs up toward her chest. "What time is it?"

"Four forty-five," I said. "The cocktail hour is at hand."

Susan shivered. She had her arms around her knees. "Maybe two aspirin," she said.

I got her some and she washed them down with the warm Diet Coke.

179

"We missed lunch," she said.

"It was worth it, I think."

"Of course it was," Susan said. "But now I need food."

"The chicken awaits," I said.

"Well done?"

"I shut it off before I swept you away to sweatered passion," I said. She smiled at me.

"You would," she said.

. . . time to disappear. He had his bag, all his stuff, time to go underground. He had a black turtleneck, black jeans, black running shoes. He adjusted the navy watch cap on his head. People would notice if he blacked his face. Two white guys had joined the black guy. They'd walked around the building and looked at all the entrances. Then the black guy left. The two white guys stayed outside. Sitting in a station wagon across from his building where they could see the front door and the side fire escape. Dumb bastards thought they had him. Nothing in this place that would help them find him. Nothing in this place anyway. Like living in a fucking toilet stall. He went out the door and down the hall and opened the back window and dropped through it maybe four feet to a roof. He ran along the roof past a window where a fat guy and his wife were on the couch watching TV and climbed the fire escape that ran up the wall of the next building. The roof door on the next building was open. Works every time. Going down the stairs in the next building, he felt the feeling in his stomach and groin. Like electricity. He had had his stuff, he was dressed for the night. Anything comes my way I can handle. On the first floor he went to

the back and out the door and down an alley, feeling the electricity in his legs, feeling the air running free into his chest. Then he was out on the next street and away in the darkness, fully equipped.

29

Susan cancelled her appointments again and sat with me in my office with Quirk, Belson, and Hawk.

"Best I can figure," Quirk said, "he went out a back window. There's a one-story addition on the back there and he must have dropped onto it and walked to the fire escape of the building next door. Then he went up, in the roof door, and down. There's a back door that leads out onto Cordis Street."

"Anything in the apartment?" I said.

"Would we search without a warrant?" Belson said.

"Yes," I said.

"Not a thing," Quirk said. "There's nothing there. A few clothes, a TV set, couple cans of tomato soup. Like no one really lived there."

"What will he do now?" I said to Susan.

"I don't know. Things will build in him. Pressure. Therapy didn't stop him from murdering before, but . . ." She shook her head.

"Couldn't you have kept him in therapy until we nabbed him?" Quirk said.

"Been good if you hadn't lost him," Hawk said. He was leaning against the wall by my window.

Quirk snapped a look at him and held it and then nodded.

He said, to Susan, "Sorry, the question was out of line."

Belson said, "Lieutenant feels like a horse's ass, losing Felton. Me too."

Susan nodded.

"Might he go for you?" Quirk said.

"He might. I have mistreated him. He feels his mother mistreated him. He would feel enormous rage. In the past when he felt it and couldn't express it directly, he would express it symbolically. How he would express his rage at me, I cannot say. Maybe he could do it directly, maybe he would have to deflect it onto something that symbolized me. There's no way to know what the symbol would be."

"So we may have less handle on him than we did before," I said.

"Before, we could figure he'd try for a black woman in her forties. Now if it's you he's trying to punish. . . ."

"I don't know," Susan said. "His symbolism is private. He could attack me, he could . . ." She shook her head. ". . . anyone," she said.

"Okay," Quirk said. "We'll start looking for him. I'm still on vacation but I can reach a lot of cops who'll look for him too."

"You have a picture?" I said.

"Yeah, got it from the security firm."

"Susan's going to stay with me," I said. "He might turn up at her place."

"We'll cover that," Quirk said. "How about the ex-wife?"

I looked at Hawk.

"Be happy to watch her," Hawk said. " 'Less you want me for backup."

"No," I said. "I'll stay close to Susan."

Hawk looked at Susan. "You be careful," he said. "You need me, you call Henry."

Susan smiled. "Yes," she said. "Thank you."

Hawk went out with Belson and Quirk.

My office was quiet.

"What do we do?" Susan said.

"Zee muzzer," I said. "We stake out zee muzzer."

"You think he'll go see his mother?" Susan said.

"Hadn't he transferred a lot of his feelings for her onto you?"

"Yes."

"So maybe if he deflects his rage, he'll deflect it at her. Possible?" I said.

"Possible," Susan said.

"Besides," I said, "I'm pretty sure he won't come here."

30

I was driving a black Jeep that year, with a hard top and all sorts of accessories that would have made the one I drove in Korea blush. Susan and I parked up the street a little from Felton's mother's house on the shore drive opposite King's Beach in Swampscott. She had the first floor of a three-story house that had gone condo when everything else had.

"Gun in your purse?" I said to Susan.

"Yes," she said.

"Purse unzipped?"

"Yes."

"Good," I said. I had my gun in a shoulder holster under my Red Sox warm-up jacket. I had the jacket unsnapped. The weather was mid-fifties and sunny. I shut the motor off on the Jeep and sat with the window half open and the smell of the ocean coming in.

"Is this in the bodyguard manual?" Susan said. "Take woman you're protecting to look for the man you're protecting her from?"

"I thought you were protecting me," I said.

"From what?"

"From becoming so swollen with seed that I burst," I said.

"I do what I can," Susan said.

It was bright morning. Young women with small children, older women with small dogs, and now and then an old man with a cane walked along the ocean front, which stretched for several miles through Swampscott and Lynn and out along the causeway to Nahant. The street ran along the seawall. A sidewalk bordered the street and an iron fence bordered the sidewalk. Past the fence was a ten-foot drop to the beach and the ocean that rolled in from Portugal. An oil tanker moved imperceptibly along the horizon from Boston Harbor, not long out of Chelsea . Creek.

"I can't leave you alone, and I have to find Felton. So we do it together," I said.

"I know," Susan said. "If it weren't so deadly, I'd kind of like it. Makes me feel like Lois Lane."

"Well, you're with the right guy," I said.

In my rearview mirror I saw Felton. He turned the corner from Monument Avenue and headed along the shore drive on my side of the street, carrying a small blue gym bag. He was dressed all in black and looked like an extra in a Rambo movie.

"Felton," I said. "He'll walk right past you, lean over and kiss me."

Susan had great reflexes. She was leaning across from her seat and her face covered mine as Felton went past on the sidewalk beside the Jeep. I could see him with one eye through Susan's hair. He was watchful in the exaggerated way of a kid playing war. He walked past us and turned in at his mother's house.

"Sometimes it's better to be lucky than good," I said to Susan.

Susan sat back up in the seat, looking toward Felton. "What now?"

"I don't know," I said. "What's his mother like? If he confesses, will she help him?"

"I have only his perception of her. If it's accurate, she will be solely interested in how to prevent damage to herself. If helping him would hush it up, she'd help. If turning him in would make her safe, she'd do that. Her concern with others' opinion of her seems nearly paralyzing, in her son's report of it."

"Why would he be here?" I said.

"I don't know."

"Is he likely to be especially vulnerable in front of his mother?"

"Yes," Susan said.

"Okay," I said. "He's clearly dressed up in his battle gear. He looks like the Hollywood version of a cat burglar."

Susan was watching with me as Felton went to his mother's house and went in the front door.

"He's got his gym bag. Maybe he's got clean socks and a toothbrush in there. But maybe he's got rope and tape and a thirty-eight caliber gun," I said. "If we caught him with the murder gun, we'd have him."

"It would be good to have hard evidence," Susan said.

"It would be intensely stupid to walk around carrying the murder weapon, knowing there's people after him," I said.

"It would be a way to be caught," Susan said.

"If he wants to be," I said.

"Part of him wants to be," Susan said. "It's probably what brought him to therapy. And caused him to write and make the phone calls."

"And come here, to his mother's, in the light of the midday sun," I said. "Let's go in."

"And then what?"

"We'll see what develops," I said.

"Do we have the right, in front of his mother?"

"Suze, up to now I've played mostly your game. But now we're in my park. Now we do it my way," I said.

"Because?"

"Because I know more about this than you do. Because this is what *I* do."

Susan was silent for a moment, looking at Felton's mother's house.

"And maybe," I said, "he's come with the rope and the gun for his mother."

Susan nodded slowly and opened the door on her side.

31

The front door opened into a small hallway with tan figured wallpaper. Stairs led straight up to the second floor.
To the right was a small dining room with a mahogany
table, two corner cabinets. To the left was a living room
that ran the depth of the house and was papered in beige
with large red flowers. Felton sat toward the back in a
bright red velvet wing chair. His mother sat on the sofa,
which was covered with a floral throw.

"Well, who's this?" Mrs. Felton said. She was a sharp-
faced little woman, her hair tightly permed and colored a
honey-brown. She had on a gray-green dress and green
high-heeled shoes.

"My name is Spenser, Mrs. Felton. And this is Dr. Silverman."

Mrs. Felton frowned a little at the Dr. Silverman. Doctors were male. And Silverman sounded Jewish. Felton

was absolutely motionless in his chair. The gym bag was on the floor at his feet. He looked at a point in space somewhere between me and Susan.

"What do you want?" Mrs. Felton said. "You should have knocked."

"Do you know what your son's been up to, Mrs. Felton?" I said. Soaping windows? Peeking in the girls' locker room, putting a tack on the teacher's chair? Her face got hard and the lines became immobile and her eyes slitted. She turned toward Felton.

"What does he mean, Gordon? What have you done now?"

Felton remained rigid and still and not looking at any of us. "Nothing," Felton said. "I don't know them."

"Dr. Silverman is your son's psychotherapist," I said.

The lines in her face deepened and the face got icy.

"Psych—?" she said.

"Psychotherapist," I said. "Dr. Silverman is a psychologist. She had been treating your son."

Mrs. Felton's features were so pinched that they seemed centered in her face.

"What did he say?"

"About you?" I smiled. "It's pretty long to summarize."

"Gordon, what have you been telling about me?"

Felton maintained his rigidity.

"I don't hold with all that psychologic business. Most of those doctors are crazier than the patients."

"Surely, you would know," I said.

We all waited. The silence was very forceful. I had no idea where I was going. I just wanted us all together there in a stressful environment for as long as I could keep us. If

191

I pushed too hard, Felton would probably bolt. If I searched his bag too soon and found clean socks and a toothbrush, it would score one for Felton, and I didn't want his psyche scoring any. If I came right out and told his mother what he was, she might faint, or throw a wing-ding, or simply deny it and order us out. That too would prop Felton up.

We were still standing just inside the living room, me forward, Susan slightly back of me. There was a back door from the living room, which probably led to the kitchen. But Felton would have to get up from his chair and go around it to reach the kitchen. Probably a back door out from the kitchen. If he could make it before I stopped him, I'd lost more steps than I thought I had.

"Gordon," Mrs. Felton said. "Just what is this business?"

"Nothing," Felton said. His voice was flat, and nearly lost somewhere back in his throat.

"Well, I'll tell you one thing," Mrs. Felton said. "No boy had a better mother. I never left him for a minute. I was always there when there was trouble. I stood on my head for this boy all his life."

I looked at Felton.

"That right, boy?"

Felton seemed to come back from wherever he was. He looked away from the fixed point in space and refocused on Susan.

"See," he said. "See what she's like?"

"Gordon," his mother said, "what on earth are you say-ing? Don't you dare speak to me that way."

Felton was still looking at Susan.

192

"Was I speaking to her?" he said. "No, I was speaking to you. But she says I shouldn't speak to her that way."

"Gordon, don't you dare," his mother said.

"See?" Felton said. He was smiling slightly. "It's good you came here, Doctor. Now maybe you'll believe me about her."

I looked at Susan and made a very slight headshake. Susan was silent.

"Gordon, that's enough. If you're in some kind of trouble, I want to hear about it. And I don't want any more fresh talk."

Felton turned and looked at her slowly, his body motionless, only his head moving. He held the look.

"Aw, Ma," he said, "fuck you."

She rocked backwards as if the phrase were physical, all the blood drained from her face. She spoke in a whisper. "What?"

Felton stood up suddenly.

"Just fuck off, will you. You been saying how you stood on your fucking head for me all my fucking life and I don't want to hear it anymore. Dr. Silverman knows. You stood me on my head. You didn't love me. You never loved anybody. You loved me when I did stuff you liked and didn't love me when I did stuff you didn't like, and none of it had any logic. You frigid bitch, you ruined my life, that's what you did."

I felt like cheering, except it was too late. The short, happy life of Gordon Felton. His mother seemed not to have heard him.

"Gordon, you may not use that language in my house.

You'll have to leave. And you'll have to take your friends with you."

She sat very straight.

"Language?" Felton's smile had widened. "Language? You mean like 'fuck you'?" He stared at her. "You know what I've done?" he said.

"Gordon, I'm your mother. You do what I say."

"You know what I've done?" Felton said again. "You know the Red Rose killer?" His face was bursting with mirth and pleasure. His cheeks were flushed. "Huh? You know that guy, Ma? Guy ties up colored girls and shoots them in the snatch?"

Mrs. Felton turned and looked firmly at the inexpensive tole lamp at the end of the couch.

Felton threw his arms wide, his face alight with laughter. "Ma, that's me. I did that, Ma. How do you like them apples, huh, Ma? Your boy Gordon is famous."

His mother whirled around at him.

"Shush," she hissed. "You just shush, this minute. I don't want to hear another word. I have friends to think of. You don't care what you do to me, do you?"

"What I do to you, Blackie? I'm the fucking serial killer, Blackie, and you did it to me."

"Don't call your mother by her first name," she said. "I refuse to listen." She resumed her examination of the lamp.

Felton stood with his arms apart, his chest heaving, the smile beginning to narrow. His mother gazed steadfastly at the lamp. He looked at her staring away from him and shook his head once. He looked at Susan.

"You?" he said.

Susan shook her head slowly.

Felton stared at her and his eyes slowly filled with tears. He shook his head again and shifted his wet gaze at me.

"So, Big Daddy," he said. "It's you and me."

"What's in the bag, Gordon?" I said.

His eyes dropped. He'd forgotten it. He looked back up at me.

"My stuff," he said.

His face remained teary, but it began to be shrewd.

"You got a warrant?" he said. His eyes began to move around the room.

I took my gun out from under my arm.

"Right here," I said.

Mrs. Felton saw the gun. Apparently she wasn't as fixated on the lamp as she looked.

"Jesus, Mary, and Joseph," she said.

I walked across the living room and picked up the gym bag from the floor between Felton's feet. I handed it to Susan. She unzipped it. "There's some duct tape, clothesline, and a revolver," she said, "and some of those sanitary gloves made out of saran wrap or whatever." I was looking at Felton. He stared back at me, the tears still muddling his eyes.

"Gotcha," I said.

Felton smiled faintly. He shrugged his shoulders. From the couch his mother hissed at him.

"Run."

He looked at her as if she'd appeared from the skies.

"Run, Gordon. We'll say they're lying. No one will know."

"Ma . . ."

195

"Run," she hissed. Her voice seemed hoarse, almost guttural.

"Run, run, run, run . . ."

"The gun will convict him, Mrs. Felton," I said.

"It won't. They don't have to know. They don't."

She stood up from the couch and walked to her son.

"Would you put me through this," she hissed. "For God's sake, run." She shoved herself suddenly between us. I put one hand on her shoulder. She slapped Felton in the face hard.

"Run, you rotten brat."

Felton gave her a look of such horror that it made my throat close. He whirled and dashed for the kitchen. His mother grabbed hold of my gun hand.

"Run," she screamed. "Run, run, run, run, run."

I shoved her out of the way and looked at Susan. She had her gun out too. Goddamn.

"I'll be fine," she said. "Get him."

I went out the back door after Felton.

32

Felton was across the drive when I rounded the corner. He went down the stairs to the beach. I jammed the gun back in the shoulder holster and snapped the safety strap as I went across the drive after him. When I reached the stairs he was a hundred yards up the beach toward Nahant. I settled into a fast jog on the damp sand. My goal was to keep him in sight.

The wind off the water was fresh and we were running into it. No world record today. The sand, as I ran, moved and reorganized under my feet and I could feel it in my shins. Felton gained a little on me. I was not perturbed. I knew I could run ten miles, maybe more, and I figured I'd outlast him. Ten miles from here and we'd be five miles out to sea. I could feel the sweat begin to form inside my shirt. As I ran I slipped out of my Red Sox jacket and let it fall on the sand. A guy walking a German Shepherd stared at the gun in its shoulder holster.

The sand was tough. I was heavier than Felton and the more weight it bore, the more the sand shifted and turned as I ran. Ahead of me Felton seemed to float above it, his feet barely reaching down to touch the ground. I lumbered on, fighting the sand, feeling the heavy Colt slapping and bouncing against my rib cage under my left arm. Ahead the beach was interrupted by a mass of tumbled boulders. Felton went up onto the boulders, and started around the promontory. He was out of sight around it by the time I reached the first rock. It was massed with seaweed and barnacles. The whole tumble of rocks was a kind of rusty color and the edges had been rounded by the continuous washing of salt water. I was careful as I climbed among the rocks. It was low tide. At high tide most of the rocks were underwater. The seaweed was wet. Perfect for clambakes; as footing, less so. A wave bigger than the others broke against the rocks, and spray tingled down on me. I steadied myself as I rounded the point of the promontory. Barnacles scraped my hand. Another big wave broke. More salt spray. It was grand work, out in the fresh air, smelling the surf, exercising vigorously.

Ahead of me the beach returned. Felton had reached it and was hot-footing along it. He glanced back at me as I dropped off a boulder and hit the sand. Felton put it into another gear, sprinting, as the gap between us widened. If he could keep that up, he'd be gone soon. I was beginning to feel pretty good. My legs were loosening and the muscles in my chest and back began to soften a little as I ran, steadily, getting a little more used to the sand. I would have shin splints tomorrow, but right now the muscles were rocking easy in vernal heat.

Felton stumbled ahead of me. The sand was no help to him either. He looked back and saw me still there and put his head down and moved out even faster. Why he took the route was a puzzle. If he'd stayed on the sidewalk and sprinted up into the neighborhoods that rise from the shoreline, he would probably have lost me by now. He was at least 150 yards out ahead. On the other hand, sweet reason had not been the guiding force for Felton up to now, and there was no reason to expect that it would suddenly appear. He'd run, probably, like an animal, toward the open light. I felt the air going in and out in large, easy breaths, sharp with the smell of the ocean. I felt like a beer commercial. Chasing a murderous psychopath along the verge of the restless sea. *It doesn't get any better than this, Gordie.* Maybe when I caught him we could exchange high fives and look at beer without drinking it. Ahead of us another promontory, more boulders, a jutt; Felton was still on my side of it. A good sign. Here the boulders reached higher up the seawall and those near the top were dry and clear of seaweed. I went up onto the boulders more easily this time. My rhythm was in synch. Higher, above the wet line, I jumped from boulder to boulder, moving only a little slower than I had running on the beach. The big waves threw a little spray but most of it hit below me as the waves broke against the rocks. When we rounded the promontory and started down toward the beach again, Felton looked like he was starting to labor. He was scrambling on the rocks with hands and feet, and when he got close to the beach he half jumped and fell onto the sand. By the time I hit the beach, Felton was only seventy-five yards ahead and his pace had slowed. He turned again to look at me. I was picking up speed. And ahead a long, unbroken stretch of beach curved gradually along the seawall for a couple of miles at least. *Better be in shape, Gordie.* As I ran now there was a kind of music to it. *Big wheel keep on turning.* To my left the ocean stretched away into space with its illusion of empty freedom. Maybe Felton's last illusion as he fled along it. Infinitely open, and yet if we turned into it, we died. *Proud Mary keep on burning.* Ahead of me Felton stumbled and fell, sprawling forward on the sand. He was scrambling as he hit and was back up and running, but in the process he lost another ten yards and I kept pumping. *Rolling on the seashore.*

Felton was running in a kind of rolling motion, heaving like a horse. His pace was uneven, and his arms were beginning to swing erratically. I closed to sixty yards. To fifty-five. To fifty. A half mile down the empty beach was the last promontory, surrounded by its jumble of sea-washed boulders. Felton looked back at me again and looked to his right where the blank seawall cut him off from the street above. He hit a particularly soft spot in the sand and pitched forward, stumbling without falling. He looked back at me. His mouth was open and his chest was heaving. I could see him blowing his breath out like sprinters do when they get anaerobic. He almost stopped. Then he lunged ahead toward the rocks. By the time he reached them he'd widened the gap again by maybe five yards. He started up them. His arms and legs moved out of concert, as if they were separately controlled. He sprawled more than he climbed, scraping along the crusty rocks, heading not only up, but out, toward the sea. I was behind him, feeling almost airborne as I went up the rocks, flexible and elastic. The Amazing Spider Man. This was the highest cluster and the one that spilled farthest out into the water. Felton was laborious now, grappling over the rocks as he went seaward. He didn't look back. He seemed eminently intent on short-range goals. Get over this rock. Don't slip into that crevice. I came behind him. Slower now. Easy. He was no longer running away. I didn't know what he was doing, but he was going to a place where there was no other place to go. Another minute of gasping struggle and he made it. Whatever *it* was for him. He was surrounded on three sides by the sea, the tide on the way in, the water driven by the tide boiling among the boulders fifty feet below. He slumped against a big, flat boulder that had tilted, in another age, onto its side, so that its flat plane made an angle maybe 30 degrees off the vertical. His back was to the boulder, his legs braced wide in front of him, his arms by his sides, palms against the rock face. His breathing was harsh and desperate and complicated by the fact that he was crying.

I walked along the sloping top of the boulders with the wind blowing strong in my face. Herring gulls roosting in the rocks flared up and circled and settled back down a bit further away. Finally I was six feet from Felton and I stopped. His face was streaked with tears and sweat. He had scratched himself on the rocks and there was blood on his hands and forearms and a little on his face. No sound came from him other than the agonized harmony of his sobbing attempts to get his breath.

Riding above the other sounds, behind me, I could hear

the high sound of sirens. Susan would have called the cops. It was a long way back, however. Out of the spray, off the rocks, on shore, where footing seemed more secure.

"Hello, hare," I said.

He looked at me and through me and beyond the rocks and shoreline. He was looking at things I'd never see, things maybe no one should have to see, and he gazed at them as his breath rasped in and out and the tears flowed down his face and his chest heaved.

"We gotta go," I said.

The sirens were still riding on the wind, but they were fewer, and already some of the police cars were on the park above the rocks, the blue lights turning, the radios making the flat noises police radios make. Mechanical voices speaking of life's darkest side. I didn't look. I knew what it looked like. I'd seen it too much, and seen lives driven into a corner too much, and done some of the driving too much.

"Shoot me," Felton gasped.

I shook my head.

"You know . . . what'll . . . happen me . . . in jail."

I nodded.

Felton looked down at the roiling water among the rocks.

"If . . . I jump . . . you . . . stop me?"

I shook my head. I looked down at the water.

"Should take you a while to die, though," I said.

Felton's breath was starting to come back. The crying hadn't stopped, but, because he could breathe a little easier, it didn't seem as frantic. He was looking at me now, his eyes a little more focused.

"I'm crazy, you know?" he said.

"Yes," I said.

"They'll put me in Bridgewater or someplace," he said. "They'll help me."

"Probably," I said. "I think they got seven hundred inmates and one shrink at Bridgewater. Might be a little different from the help you're used to."

The spray was kicking higher as the tide rose. I was damp with it. My hair was flat to my skull, my face was wet. My breathing was nearly normal and my heart rate was back under a hundred and I felt the easy passage of blood in my veins. Couple of cold beers would be grand right now, maybe a friendly chat with someone who hadn't murdered four women. Behind me, from the park, someone with a bullhorn said, "This is the Lynn Police, do you need assistance?"

I raised my hand without looking around and waved them away.

"It was her," Felton said. "She made me like this. I had to be like this."

I shrugged.

"Come on," I said. "We gotta go."

"I can't," Felton said.

"I'll help you," I said.

I stepped toward him and took his arms and pulled him from the rock. His legs gave way and he sagged. I slid my arms under his arms and around his back and held him up. He sagged toward me and buried his face in my chest and began to cry harder. His arms went around me and held me and he was saying something muffled against my chest. I listened harder.

"Papa," he sobbed. "Papa."

I held him there for a long time, feeling pity and revulsion in nearly equal parts, until two Lynn cops climbed out and the three of us brought him in.

33

Susan was eating sushi in the new Suntory restaurant in Boston. She ate it with chopsticks, managing them as easily as I did the fork I'd had to request.

"Jesus," I said, "that fish isn't even cooked."

"Shall I send it back?" Susan said.

I was having some vegetable tempura, and the house beer.

"Best not to offend the chef," I said. "He's still got to cook my shrimp."

"Okay," Susan said. "Then I'll choke it down."

She took a small sip of saki. Then she gestured with the cup. "Marathon man," she said. And smiled.

"The race goes not always to the swift," I said.

"I've seen you shoot," Susan said. "You could have shot him as he ran."

"Probably," I said. "Pretty sure I could have hit him when he climbed the rocks."

"But you didn't," she said.

I shrugged. Susan smiled a little wider.

"I know why you didn't," she said.

"Yeah?"

I ate some more tempura, unashamedly, with my fork.

"The first time you chased him he outran you and got away," Susan said.

"Well, there was this fence," I said.

"And this time," Susan said, "you were going to chase him and catch him."

"To even it up?" I said. "Come, now. Doesn't that sound pretty childish?"

"Absolutely," Susan said.

"Smart-ass shrink," I said.

Susan ate another morsel of sushi, looking satisfied. "Quirk and Belson back from vacation?" Susan said.

"Yeah."

"Any apologies?" Susan said.

I grinned. "Not hardly," I said. "Everybody is reminding everybody else that they agreed with Quirk right along."

"What about the man they accused?"

"Washburn? They'll try him for the murder of his wife."

"And Gordon Felton?"

"I assume he'll plead insanity, the court will believe him, and he'll go to Bridgewater State Hospital. Where he will not be cured."

"Well, without arguing about legal insanity, Felton probably couldn't not have done what he did," Susan said.

"And yet," I said, "there's lots of people who grow up

with the kind of problems Felton had and they don't go out and kill a bunch of women."

"I don't know," Susan said. "I mean, I could say some competent-sounding thing about the infinite number of variables in the human circumstance, so that no two people in fact grow up with the same kinds of problems. But that's really only another way of saying 'I don't know.'"

"Can he be cured?"

"Not at Bridgewater," Susan said.

"I know that," I said. "But under the right circumstances is he curable?"

Susan took her last bite of sushi, and a swallow of saki. "Cure is probably the wrong word. He can be helped. He can probably be prevented from getting worse, maybe he can be relieved of the pressures that drive him to act out his pathology, maybe he can be redirected, so to speak, so that he acts out in less destructive ways."

"Is this going to be on the final?" I said.

"I know it sounds so shrinky, but it's the only real answer I have. The other thing that enters into the question of cure is, of course, the severity of what he does. If his pathology manifested itself by, say, stealing pantyhose off the clothesline, maybe you could say, yes, he can be cured. Because if you're wrong, the consequences are trivial. But how can anyone certify that when released he will not murder someone? No, I certainly could not."

The waitress came and took our plates and brought us some shrimp tempura and steamed rice. She brought me another beer. When she was gone I said to Susan, "I feel kind of bad for Felton."

Susan said, "Yes."

207

"I feel even worse for the women he murdered."

"Yes," Susan said again. "How about his mother?"

"That's hard," I said.

"But not impossible," Susan said. "Think how desperately she's had to manipulate her life without any power but the uses of love."

"And all for naught," I said. "Her reputation will be smirched anyway."

"Cruel," Susan said.

"Well, I never had a mother," I said. "Probably makes me insensitive."

"Probably," Susan said, "but you've got strong loins. It makes up for a lot."

I reached over and poured more saki from the warm bottle into the little saki cup.

"You know what I like about this whole business?" I said.

"Not much," Susan said.

"I liked you and me," I said.

Susan nodded.

"I always like you and me," I said, "but this time had such potential for us being a mutual pain in the ass that I especially admire us because we weren't."

"Yes," Susan said, "we were continuously in each other's way trying to do our business."

"And we didn't get mean about it," I said. "We were kind to each other all the time."

"Most of the time," Susan said.

"Close enough," I said.

Susan smiled at me and put her hand on top of mine as it rested on the table.

"It was a charged situation," she said. "You telling me what to do in my profession and me telling you what to do in yours. And both of us a little weird about our autonomy."

"Without endorsing the *us,*" I said, "let me suggest a suitable reward for being so integrated."

"I do not want to go to Fenway Park and watch the Red Sox do anything," Susan said.

"I had in mind exotic sexual congress," I said.

"With the Red Sox?"

"After last year, I think they're too clumsy," I said. "I was thinking that you deserve me, Foots Spenser."

"Yes," Susan said, "God help me, I'm afraid that's just what I deserve."

"So," I said, "shall we finish dinner, go back to your place, and make love?"

"Certainly," Susan said.

"With or without sweater?" I said.

There was a long, silent moment while Susan looked at me, straight on. Her great dark eyes wide, her face wearing an odd expression that might have been a smile. Then she did something I've never seen her do. Something, perhaps, that no one had ever seen her do.

She blushed.

. . . It was hot in the cell. And the jail was loud, full of angry obscene shouts. He had never been in jail before. There was no light in the cell. He could see the bright lights in the hall that made long shadows. The smell was bad too. Urine, shit, steam pipes, body odor, cigarettes, fear. There was no one in the cell with him. This was an angry, frightened male world, dark and fetid and womanless. Already they knew. Prisoners yelled at him when he came in. The blacks looked at him every step he took past them. He cried, lying on the bare mattress, his face in his arms. No one cared. No one. He was entirely alone. His aloneness ached in him, deep into his stomach and up his throat and along the backs of his arms. He felt weak and tiny. No one. Nobody. No one . . . He remembered lying in his mother's bed . . . the last thing, the thing he hadn't told the shrink. His mother's body, naked, smelling a little like cooking, touching him. Her hand pressing, touching, the smell of white wine, his mother's sounds, voiceless, wordless sounds as she forced him against her. Into her. He sat up on the bed and took off his shirt. He knotted one sleeve around his neck and stood and walked to the cell door and put one foot on a crossbar and stepped up, holding himself by a forearm looped through the bars. He fumbled the other sleeve up through the bars and tied it to a crosspiece with his free hand,

guided by the hand hooked through the bars. He snugged the sleeve tight so there was maybe a foot of play and turned, holding himself with both hands.

"I never told," he said. He heard the voice in the empty cell and heard it echo in the personless dark. "I never told, Momma," he said, and freed his feet from the crosspiece and let go with his hands. . . .